ANNIE'S SUMMER

ALICE SHOEMAKER

Illustrations by Scott Shoemaker

Fairgreen Press
Indianapolis

Additional copies may be ordered from:

Fairgreen Press, Indianapolis

317-767-4894

Dedication

To my parents Charles and Alva Eby Amick, who took me into their home and hearts

and

to Robert L. Shoemaker, loving husband and father

Chapter One

Annie's New Puppy

Summer vacations began early in Wakarusa—in April. On Annie's first Monday off, she went with her father to make house calls to those people who were too sick or too feeble to come to his office in town and pick up some pills or a bottle of syrupy medicine.

The windows of her father's green Ford were rolled all the way down that spring day in 1936 even though the dust and grit from the washboard gravel road enveloped them. Outside, the trees were just beginning to leaf with delicate fringe. Some had miniature pale-green leaves that reminded her of the tiny paper umbrellas Cousin John had sent along in his last letter to her parents. Down the road, farmers were plowing their fields. Annie watched as the color of earth changed from deep moist black in the wake of the farmer's plow to lighter brown in the furrows farther away.

"Annie," her father said, "when you're older and learn how to drive, you'll see that you have to go forty or faster over these gravel roads, otherwise you hit each individual ridge." Annie couldn't wait to be older and do all the things grown-ups did.

From the washboard road, they turned up a narrow lane. Two parallel ruts led to an old farmhouse perched like a gray owl on the rise of a hill. Its unpainted boards and curtainless windows looked down on a ramshackle barn, a muddy farmyard, and a patch of scraggly grass where two boys were making a sign.

Dr. Ziegler stopped the car, took his black bag out of the back seat, and went into the farmhouse. Annie hurried over to the boys, one tall and thin, the other short and dumpy. Both were dirty.

"Watcha' doin'?" she asked.

"Makin' a For Sale sign for puppies," the taller one answered.

Sprawling in the grass were two brown pups, fat and round, rolling against each other and punctuating their play with an occasional muted bark.

Annie knelt on the grass and picked up one of the wriggling balls of fur. Placing him on his back in her lap, she cautiously touched his rough nose and wrinkled forehead. Then she stroked the sides of his smooth-as-a-peach belly with her finger. The pup's brown eyes searched her face. Finally, he closed them, and with a little snort, rolled over and fell asleep. She must have held him a long time while watching the boys—neither very talkative—work on their sign.

Suddenly, as if in answer to her prayer, a shadow fell on her and a gruff voice directed at the boys said, "How much do you want for the pup?"

The older boy thought for a moment, running his tongue back and forth in the place where his two front teeth had been, and said, "Fifteen cents."

Annie's father reached in his pocket and gave the taller boy a dime. He then handed a nickel to the younger boy, who hadn't said a word. She couldn't believe it! A dog of her own! Someone to talk to at night when her friends were home with their brothers and sisters. Looking down at his light brown head, she spotted a flea crawling through the fur towards his ear. I'll have to give him a bath, she thought. Then she chuckled to herself. "Cute as a bug's ear." That's what Nora would say when she saw him. Nora liked animals. She even liked bugs. Funny how different Nora and Mother are, thought Annie. As different as vacation and school.

Holding the puppy awkwardly in the cups of her hands, Annie climbed into the car. I'll call him Sandy, she said to herself.

Annie and her father didn't talk much. There were a lot of things she wanted to ask him, like why he and her mother argued so often. Once she did ask why she didn't have any brothers or sisters. Her father said it was because of the Depression. She knew about the Depression firsthand. It was the reason they had chicken for dinner every Sunday. Her father's patients often paid him in chickens or butter. "At least we have enough to eat," said her mother when Annie complained about having chicken again.

Silently, her father hightailed it back to Wakarusa, the Ford flying across the ridges in the road, the dust flying in the windows. He even drove through several stop signs on the way. Annie's friend Bobby had told her that people in Wakarusa kept their eyes peeled for Dr. Ziegler when he was behind the wheel. Each year when he traded in his old Ford and got a new one from Emil Schmidt, the word moved quickly through town to watch out for Doc, who was now driving a different-colored car. Bobby said they named a driving maneuver after him—a wide sweep turning right from the middle of the street was called a "Doc Ziegler Special."

Her father's wooden-frame office was a block east of the town square, next door to their red brick house. Annie and her father came into town from the west, and as they approached the office, Dr. Ziegler made a sweeping U-turn—a sort of "Reverse Special"—coming to a stop in the yellow space reserved for him directly in front of his office. He left his keys in the ignition, for he had to be ready for an emergency any time of the day or night, and in Wakarusa there were plenty of them.

Carrying Sandy carefully, Annie hurried out of the

car into her father's office. There she found Nora, her father's nurse, sitting at his roll-top desk doing crossword puzzles.

"Nora, Nora, look what I have!"

Nora took the pup into her arms and smiled at him. "Why, he's as cute as a bug's ear. See, he's sticking out his tongue and licking my finger. He must be thirsty."

Handing Sandy back to Annie, Nora got up from the desk, walking carefully in order not to bump her thick, swollen legs. As far back as Annie could remember, Nora's legs had been that way, with the flesh where her ankles should be hanging over the tops of her shoes like newly baked bread over the edge of the pan.

Annie stole a glance at the windows of her house next door. She felt certain she saw the curtains move, and her stomach tightened. Then her mother, who had probably been watching sharp-eyed from one of those windows, came in the back door of Dr. Ziegler's office.

"What do you have, Annie?" she asked, her thin lips taut with disapproval.

"A puppy, Mother," Annie replied carefully, as she felt her stomach tighten another notch.

"Well, you know I don't allow animals in my house."

Nor fish, nor beer, nor flowers, Annie's mind chanted.

Every Sunday evening Annie's father would go next door to his office, open a can of sardines, and feast upon them along with some Ritz crackers and a bottle of beer. To her mother, fish smelled bad and beer was sinful.

Flowers were another matter. Annie's mother didn't want them in the house, she said, because they carried in bugs and dripped petals. But there was something else. Flowers are beautiful, and Annie suspected that her mother disliked beautiful things.

Yet an old picture of her mother had often pierced her memory. She had found it in a cedar chest, and like the pungent smell of the cedar, the image of the picture remained with her. In the picture Mrs. Ziegler's hair was piled on top of her head, and she wore a pleated blouse with a high lace-trimmed collar. Dangling from her ears were long elegant earrings. Now she wore old cotton housedresses, torn stockings, and clunky shoes. Annie wondered why her mother had changed from the beautiful woman in the picture.

Nora brought a pan of water from the back of the office, and Annie, taking Sandy and the water, hurriedly slipped out the back door. Through the screen she could hear her parents arguing.

"You know I don't like dogs, especially since that hunting dog of yours had fleas," Annie's mother said angrily.

"Now, Mrs. Ziegler," her father replied, "Annie is lonely, and I think a dog would be good company for her this summer."

"Company! Company!" she said. "She's just like you are, Doctor—always has to be entertained or on the go. Can't sit at home and amuse herself. And now she'll have that mangy animal trailing all over town with her. Besides, you know how people in town resent dogs running loose—and for good reason, too!"

There was a pause, then Annie heard her father speaking slowly and deliberately. "Well, I don't think it's fair to a dog to chain it up. Animals need freedom in order to be happy, and there's nothing so sad as a dog on a chain."

"Fair! It's not fair to me to have to clean up after that animal. All I do around here is clean up after other people. And now, Doctor, a dog!"

Annie wasn't sure why her parents never called each other by their first names. But now she had something more important to think about.

Placing Sandy carefully on the grass with his water, she kept an eye on him while she rummaged in the small woodshed behind her father's office—a catchall for the cardboard boxes that the huge medicine bottles came in. Finding one that was just the right size, she lined it with some soft shredded newspaper. Then Annie put Sandy inside and stubbornly carried him into the house and up to her room.

Her mother didn't find them there until after lunch. By then Sandy had peed on the floor at the foot of Annie's bed.

"Get that dog out of my house," Mrs. Ziegler said. "Why, when I was a child, a dog never set foot inside the house."

Some days Annie argued with her, but today she knew better. Quickly mopping up the puddle, she put Sandy into his box and took him outside to the woodshed.

There she sat on the dirty floor of the shed holding him in her lap. Forgetting all of the evenings when her mother had read bedtime stories to her and the closeness she had felt to her then, Annie asked Sandy, "Why does she act like this? It's just like school with grown-ups giving orders all the time. I hate that!"

Chapter Two

The Town Park

May. The red and yellow tulips in Dr. Ziegler's flower bed were in full bloom, and the crab apple trees were almost ready for what Nora called Pink Cloud Day. Annie lay in bed wondering what time it was. The light, pale and gold, came through the white muslin curtains, which moved gently in the breeze from the open windows. She could smell the crab apple blossoms outside and hear their branches rasping back and forth on the roof.

Reaching under the covers, she found Sandy, who yawned sleepily. He was housebroken now, so every night, after her parents were in bed, she'd tiptoe downstairs and out the back door to the woodshed to get him and bring him upstairs. Once her mother heard her and called from her parents' downstairs bedroom to ask what she was doing. "Just getting milk from the ice box," Annie said. In a way that was true, for Sandy had developed a fondness for milk.

Although she didn't have a clock in her room or own a watch, Annie could usually tell time by the early morning sounds she heard. Her father's coughing—he smoked two packs of cigarettes a day—told her it was 7:15. Her parents' arguing meant it was eight and they were having breakfast. Today the house was still.

Good, she thought. I'll put Sandy outside and fix some breakfast. After dressing hurriedly, she coaxed Sandy out of bed, and they went downstairs.

Out of loyalty to Jack Armstrong, the All-American Boy, Annie always had Wheaties for breakfast. Along with her cereal, she drank Ovaltine, a chocolate mixture put into milk. The latter product was very important because she was saving Ovaltine labels for a Little Orphan Annie Code Captain's Belt, and she almost had enough.

Both Bobby Myers, who lived across the street, and she had Orphan Annie badges, but only he had a red, white, and blue-striped Code Captain's belt with its secret inscription embossed behind the gold metal buckle, and he wouldn't tell her what the code was. Annie felt she could unlock the secrets of the universe if she only had that belt. Two more labels to go, she thought, as she drank another mugful.

Putting the dishes in the sink, she went out the back door. Sandy heard her, and together they walked past the tulips and the woodshed to the back door of her father's office. Her mother and father sat in the waiting room, as they often did in the morning, reading the *Chicago Tribune*, which was delivered there for the patients.

"Well, Annie, you look chipper this morning," said Nora, who had also arrived at the office and was the first to see her.

Her father looked up from reading and smiled.

"Annie, you haven't brushed your hair," said her mother. "It looks awful."

"Yes, I have," she replied, "but I was in a hurry." Actually, she had run the brush through it a time or two. "I promised Bobby and Margaret I'd meet them in the park, and I'm late."

"Well, be back in time to set the table for lunch. You know we eat at noon," her mother replied, then went back to reading her part of the *Tribune*.

Got off easy that time, Annie decided. She didn't even ask if I'd made my bed. As Annie and Sandy left the front porch of her father's office, she heard her mother complaining about some insect bites. "I don't know where I could have gotten them," Mrs. Ziegler said.

Crossing the street and heading down the alley, Annie checked out the boxes behind Goldberg's Department Store. Big boxes made good clubhouses, and Mr. Goldberg was always nice about letting Annie and her friends have anything they found behind his store.

Mr. Goldberg was one of the few Jews in Wakarusa. Annie's father once told her that Mr. Goldberg's father, Moses, had come from Russia and had started out years earlier with a horse and wagon peddling pots and pans throughout the area. Now his son, who was about fifty and her father's best friend, owned the biggest dry goods store in town.

Annie preferred Mr. Goldberg's father, who would smoke a cigarette down to the end, the ash dangling precariously, and then grind it out in the palm of his left hand. She would watch the old man's face carefully for signs of pain from the burning cigarette, but to her amazement there never were any.

Further down the alley was the back of Keever's Grocery Store. She reached in her dress pocket and pulled out a penny. Inside Mr. Keever's back door she found his grown son, whom everyone called Harold, behind the meat counter. When he wasn't working in the store, Harold was the town marshal, but since there had never yet been any crime in Wakarusa, he was everybody's friend.

Harold did have to use his revolver once two years ago when Amos Frederick's dog staggered onto the town square with a beard of foam drooling out of its mouth. Annie shuddered as she remembered first her fear and then the pitiable sight of the dog as it wobbled unsteadily to the center of the street. After the initial sighting of the animal, all traffic stopped, and the townspeople stood back with hushed voices while someone ran to get Harold. He came, revolver in hand.

By this time Spot had collapsed on the pavement. The marshal walked to within ten feet of the helpless animal, aimed, and pulled the trigger. "A shot in the head. Best cure for rabies there is," said old John Sayers. Annie didn't like the red-faced bearded man from that time on.

Now, at the meat counter, Annie said, "May I have a penny's worth of dried beef?"

"Sure, Annie," said Harold, and he patiently took a large hunk of meat from the refrigerated case. Using the electric slicer, he allowed four thin pieces of the salty red meat to fall on a sheet of waxed paper. Then with a smile, he handed them to her. Annie gave him a penny and went out the back door munching the meat—all but one slice, which she gave to Sandy, who had been waiting.

Opposite to the Goldbergs' and Keevers' back doors, on the east side of the alley, was the Karschmans' garden and barn. There the sweet peas were already in bloom, climbing up carefully constructed trellises, while rows of green leaf lettuce were appearing, along with some other seedlings she didn't recognize.

Behind the Karschmans' barn was a large pile of sand and to the left of that, as she looked, was the town park—a quarter of a block square with swings, monkey bars, and a two-story white stucco building—all under the leafy canopy of dozens of maple trees. It was here, according to Bobby, that Wakarusa got its name.

Long, long ago, on a cold winter's day, an Indian maiden—probably a princess—was leading her horse across ice that had recently formed in the center of what was now the park. As she wearily trudged across the ice, she suddenly broke through and sank in mud up to her knees. "Wakarusa," she cried, which means "Knee-Deep in Mud."

Well, the park was muddy, and there was Margaret in a pale yellow dress trying not to get any on her. Margaret and

Annie were good friends even though they were different. "Margaret is a little lady," Annie's mother always said. That made Annie want to throw up, but she liked Margaret in spite of her mother's opinion.

Last summer Annie had talked Mrs. Ziegler into letting Margaret stay overnight one Saturday. After dark the two girls had climbed out on the roof beneath Annie's bedroom windows and watched the farmers and their wives walk slowly back to their cars laden with the week's groceries. When the sounds of voices and footsteps faded, they rolled buckeyes down the sloping tile roof and giggled until their sides ached as the brown pellets bounced off the sidewalk below.

Annie's parents were careful not to argue that night or the next morning, but after Margaret left, they started in all over again. Annie felt lonelier than ever. She had wanted to ask Margaret if her parents argued, too, but she knew she'd feel ashamed and disloyal if she did. At least now she could talk to Sandy about it.

She hoped Margaret and she could spend the night together again this summer.

Not only did she enjoy talking and giggling with Margaret, but just last week Margaret had learned how to swear from her older brother and some time soon was going to teach her.

"Hi, Annie," Margaret said, as she brushed back a wisp of hair from her face.

Annie loved Margaret's hair. It was straight and black. Annie's was blonde and curly. Margaret had freckles on her nose. Annie's always got sunburned. But Margaret didn't have a dog, and she did.

"Where's Bobby?" Annie asked.

"He'll probably be here in a minute," Margaret replied as she petted Sandy. She knew how he liked his head rubbed in front of his ears.

Sandy saw Bobby before the girls did. He gave a bark and wagged his tail, and there Bobby was, out of breath with his shoelaces untied. "That boy never tucks in his shirttail," Annie's mother would say.

"Hey, you guys, let's try out the new swings," Bobby said.

"Sam, Sam the lavatory man, takes care of the public can," sang Bobby as the swings went back and forth. "Hands out the paper and the towels and likes. . . ."

"Race you to the pump," interrupted Margaret, who had heard the song before. The three friends jumped off the swings and ran to the south edge of the park. Margaret and Bobby, who tied for first, took turns pumping the cold well water into each other's cupped hands. Annie, who felt especially daring that day, used the tin cup hanging next to the pump.

The cup had been placed there for tramps—those unshaven, out-of-work men who roamed the countryside these Depression days looking for free food and odd jobs. As she drank the metallic-tasting water, she thought about how her mother had special dishes set aside—a cracked plate, a chipped cup, and old silverware—just for these men. She recalled seeing one of them eating his meal of scrambled eggs while sitting on the steps of her back porch. She also remembered hearing Mrs. Karschman speak to a shabby man on her back porch about how important it was to be saved. At the Karschmans' house a tramp got to use regular dishes, but they came with a sermon.

After they drank all they could hold and gave Sandy a drink, they walked over to a large pile of sand in the northwest corner of the park near an intersection of alleys. There Bobby had an idea.

"Let's level out this pile of sand and then this afternoon after lunch we can build an Indian village," he said.

So the three of them set to work, even Margaret join-ing in, scooping sand with her hand to level the pile. They were almost finished when a man with a beard came running across the vacant lot opposite the park. He was waving his hands and yelling. Annie saw that it was old John Sayers, the man who had joked about Frederick's dog being shot.

"You kids git out of here. Don't you know any better than to mess up other people's work?" Mr. Sayers, a member of the town board, was in charge of the park. His face was red and his eyes squinted together—mean and beady. He spat on the ground.

"Git out of here," he repeated, "and take that mutt with you. There's a law against animals running loose in this town!"

Annie looked at Margaret, whose eyes were wide with amazement, as if nobody had talked to her like that before. Bobby, she noticed, was trying hard not to laugh. Annie was mad. She was sick of grown-ups telling kids what and what not to do. Quickly, the three decided to go home for lunch and meet afterwards at Margaret's. Sandy and Annie, whose stomach ached, walked back up the alley together. Some day, thought Annie, I'll be grown up, and I'm going to be different.

When Annie came in the house, she heard her mother talking on the phone, a large rectangular box with a crank at-tached to the wall. Seeing Annie walk into the back hallway, Mrs. Ziegler began speaking Pennsylvania Dutch, a sort of fractured German that she and her sisters had spoken when they were children.

"Yah, gut, gut," she said in a voice that sounded strange and kind of strangled.

Annie walked back in the kitchen where her mother couldn't see her and slammed the screen door as if she were leaving, but her mother hung up the receiver anyway. Annie heard it click and then heard her mother walking into her par-ents' bedroom. Mrs. Ziegler closed the door and locked it. A moment later, as Annie drew near the door, sounds of muffled crying came from the other side.

Somehow Annie felt the phone call might be about Cousin John. Her mother really liked her nephew, this son of her sister Martha, but then so did Annie. John's job as a reporter for the *Chicago Tribune* took him to all parts of the world. Even though he was busy gathering news, he would remember to send Annie postcards and small gifts from Shanghai, Paris, Rome, and other far-off places which Annie longed to visit. Annie looked forward to receiving Cousin John's postcards and gifts, but she loved his infrequent visits even more because Cousin John treated her like an adult.

Chapter Three

Ely's Bear

"Annie, hurry and get dressed—and don't wear shorts. Aunt Martha might be at the cemetery." Mrs. Ziegler's voice startled Annie, for she had been dreaming that Sandy and she were walking through a meadow filled with flowers.

So she doesn't want me to wear shorts, huh? Might as well be back in school. Who cares about Aunt Martha? she thought. "Young ladies don't wear shorts in public," Annie said in a high nasty voice, imitating Aunt Martha as she put on a gathered skirt covered with an octopus-like design.

It was almost June. Nights were warm now, and Sandy slept outside, so Annie came down the steps alone. Her mother's eyes opened wide and her lips grew thin when Annie walked in the kitchen. "Why are you wearing that skirt? You know I don't like it."

"Well, you told me not to wear shorts," Annie replied smugly.

Mrs. Ziegler looked at her daughter strangely and then went out to the garden.

After a quick breakfast, Annie joined her mother. Silently, they cut the pale pink and magenta peonies, which were covered with ants. Mrs. Ziegler scowled at the ants as she brushed them off her fingers. Then they put the sticky, sweet flowers in glass canning jars full of water. Decoration Day was the last Sunday in May, and the flowers were for the graves of Annie's grandparents.

As they drove north towards the cemetery, Annie thought of her mother's reaction to her skirt and of her own recent discovery of her mother's fear of cancer. Mrs. Ziegler would not even use the word in the dinner-table conversations her parents often had about diseased gall bladders and enlarged kidney stones. One day when Annie and Margaret were looking through Dr. Ziegler's medical books for pictures of naked men, they found a drawing of cancer that had enlarged and spread with octopus-like tentacles. Annie was astonished to find that the pattern of the spreading cancer resembled the pattern in her skirt. She was quick to point out this similarity to her mother and began calling it her cancer skirt. Mrs. Ziegler reacted by insisting that Annie put the skirt in the pile of clothing intended for flood victims. Annie was pleased with herself for having thought to dig it out of the pile and wear it. So there.

Mother and daughter rode to the cemetery in silence, Mrs. Ziegler gripping the steering wheel and staring straight ahead. Once at the cemetery, they dug out last year's weeds and rubble, finally placing the peonies on the graves of Annie's grandparents, who had died before she was born.

In the lot next to the cemetery was Mrs. Ziegler's church, a plain building of orange brick with white-framed windows of clear glass.

"Why doesn't your church have stained-glass windows?" Annie asked her mother.

"Because Mennonites believe that stained glass is worldly," Mrs. Ziegler replied.

"Is that why you don't have an altar or a cross in the front of the church?" asked Annie.

"No. We don't have an altar or a cross because the Bible says not to worship graven images."

"What about the clock?"

Her mother gave her a quick look. "That's there to tell

time. Besides, it's not at the front of the church but on the wall at the side."

"There's lots to keep track of in your church," said Annie, wondering what it had to do with God.

While her mother talked to friends and relatives who were also decorating graves, Annie walked around the cemetery reading the messages engraved on old tombstones. One in particular raised goose bumps on her arms. Carved on its granite surface were the words

I was once like you
You will someday be like me

She quickly walked back to the car, being careful not to step on someone's grave.

On the way back to Wakarusa, Mrs. Ziegler seemed to be in a better mood, and Annie was beginning to feel sorry that she had worn the skirt.

"Have you ever noticed how much richer the dirt is in Elkhart County than in St. Joe?" Mrs. Ziegler asked as they drove by fields filled with newly emerging corn.

Annie admitted she hadn't.

"It's because Elkhart County is Republican," Mrs. Ziegler said.

"You mean that God likes Republicans better than Democrats?"

"Of course," Mrs. Ziegler answered.

Annie thought that was a dumb idea. That would mean that God didn't like President Roosevelt, and her father was planning to vote for Mr. Roosevelt in November. But then, Annie realized, Father doesn't believe in God.

Annie and her father went to the Methodist church in town, where Reverend Crumly was a good friend of her father's. Annie once asked her father what he thought about

God, and he said he wasn't sure.

"Then why do we go to church?" she asked.

"Because you need to learn about religion," he answered.

Annie thought it was strange that her mother, who believed in God, stayed home on Sunday to answer the telephone in case of emergencies, but her father, who didn't believe in God, took her to the Methodist church every Sunday. Well, she could add that to her list of things to wonder about.

She still hadn't figured out exactly why her mother had been crying behind the closed door of her parents' bedroom, but that afternoon one of Mrs. Ziegler's sisters called, and mixed in with the Pennsylvania Dutch were the words "John"—"needs the operation"—and "Mayo Clinic." Annie thought of John and how she always was glad to hear from him. When she recalled the anxious tone of her mother's voice, she felt a twinge in her stomach.

Later that afternoon Annie reluctantly climbed the thirty-two steps to Dr. Myers's dental office. She dreaded every one, for it was time to have her teeth cleaned, and Dr. Myers always discovered lots of cavities.

At the top of the steps she turned left and went down a dark hallway towards the dentist's waiting room. On one side of the hallway were two doors leading into upstairs apartments where people lived. A third door, which was open, led into the bathroom that Dr. Myers's patients could use. Annie had never seen a bathroom like this one, with the toilet mounted on two raised, step-like platforms, so that by the time a person ascended them, her head was almost touching the ceiling. When Annie read about kings or queens, she often imagined that their thrones would be on platforms similar to this. For that reason she always used the bathroom whether she had to or not.

Usually she had to, though, because going to the dentist made her uneasy, and the little sign in Dr. Myers's waiting room didn't help:

Just one life will soon be past,
Only what's done for Christ will last.

There it was, tacked on the wall next to the door leading from the waiting room into the dentist's inner office.

Annie chose the chair farthest from the sign. From her seat on the other side of the room, she could hear the voices of Dr. Myers and his assistant Pearl—who had pearly white teeth—talking to the person in the dental chair. Occasionally, she heard a grunt or a garbled response, which she supposed was the person in the chair. At least he or she wasn't yelling or moaning.

Only one other person was in the waiting room. It was Tom Braden, with a pile of rabbit skins over one arm. He scowled when he saw Annie. She pretended not to notice him as he turned his back and looked out the window on the town square below. Once his back was to her, she studied his skillfully patched pants and home-cut hair curiously.

Tom was a sophomore at Wakarusa High School and would probably quit school as soon as he was sixteen. Recently, Annie had overheard her parents say that Mr. Braden had been laid off from his factory job in Elkhart. Only last winter Bobby had warned her and Margaret not to go in the field east of the park because Tom set traps there for rabbits. Bobby said that every time Tom caught one, his family could have rabbit stew for dinner. When Bobby finished, Margaret added that her brother wasn't allowed to hang around with Tom or his brother Joe.

"Is it because they're poor?" asked Bobby.

"Everybody's poor in this town," replied Margaret,

closing the subject.

Tom stood studying the scene below until Dr. Myers appeared in the door of the waiting room and said, "Tom, I can see you now for just a minute."

Turning abruptly, Tom walked into Dr. Myers's office.

Annie thought it strange to see the angry-faced teenager holding the rabbit skins so carefully.

"Well, if it isn't Annie, the little French Princess," said the dentist, noticing her. Bobby's father liked to tease, and that made visits to his office almost bearable. "I'll be just a minute or two. Tom has something he wants to show me."

Why in the world was Tom Braden carrying rabbit skins into the dentist's office?

Through the closed door she heard Dr. Myers say, "Well, Tom, I can't pay for the silver and gold I've put in your mother's teeth with rabbit skins." There was a long pause. "But I will take four of them," the dentist said.

Annie and her friends all looked forward to summer Saturday nights in Wakarusa. This Saturday the band was playing a special program in honor of Flag Day, probably a kind of dress rehearsal for the Fourth of July concert.

Margaret met Annie in front of the bandstand, as they had planned. The clarinets—with the exception of Amy Shroeder's, which kept squeaking—were already leading the way with "Pomp and Circumstance" when the girls arrived.

"Did you bring it?" Annie asked Margaret, giggling with excitement.

"No, we didn't have any. Did you bring one?" Margaret asked.

"No, and Harold didn't have any to sell," Annie replied disappointedly.

"Oh, heck!"

"Maybe a lemon wouldn't work for a trombone player

anyway," Annie said.

"Maybe," Margaret replied without conviction.

"Let's try making faces at him," Annie said. So the two girls moved to the side of the raised platform where the brass section was seated and found Bobby, hair combed and shirt tucked in place, concentrating fiercely on the music while moving the slide of his trombone to its destined position.

"I wonder how he knows where to put the slide," Annie said.

"I can't hear you. It's too noisy here," Margaret shouted.

They edged through the throngs of people towards the arresting aroma of Mr. Ferguson's popcorn stand.

Although only about a thousand people lived in the town itself, many farmers from the surrounding area would put on freshly laundered overalls and, along with their wives and children, would come to Wakarusa on Saturday night. The entire family had worked hard in the fields all week and by the weekend were ready for a treat. Now they scattered—the men to the barber shop to catch up on the latest news and the women and small children to Goldberg's and Keever's to do the weekly shopping.

Sprinkled among the crowd were the Amish. Instead of denim overalls, Amish men wore black broadcloth suits, white shirts, and broad-brimmed hats. The women, whose dresses of Easter-egg colors were all made alike, wore white net hats—which looked like tea strainers and were called coverings—perched on the tops of their heads. The children were dressed like miniature adults minus the black hats and coverings.

Annie looked about her, taking in the colorful dresses of lavender, blue, and turquoise, the sounds of the band, the smell of the popcorn, and the laughing, talking people. As she crunched on her popcorn and wiped her greasy fingers on her skirt, she said to herself that this was the way life ought to be.

"I've got an idea," Margaret said, as the girls ate their popcorn and watched the crowd.

"What is it?" Annie asked, always ready to try something new.

"Let's buy some more popcorn and take it to Ely's bear."

"Good," Annie replied, reaching into her skirt pocket and coming up with a nickel. "Here's my half."

They bought the popcorn and left the crowds, the light, and the music, walking north of the square through the near darkness.

"By the way, where's Sandy?" Margaret asked.

"He snapped at Mr. Sayers when he walked by our house today, and my mother made me tie him up," said Annie.

"Well, he and the bear might not get along."

Fireflies flashed on and off—dots of phosphorous against the approaching darkness—as the girls ambled along towards Ely's Farm Implement Store across from the school. Their eyes grew accustomed to the blueness of the night. The sound of the band faded in the background; instead, Annie heard water running in the town ditch nearby, and she smelled sewage mixed in with the smell of honeysuckle. Then she saw the bear—its blackness silhouetted against the dark blue sky. It was chained to a post. Nearby was a barrel and a large pan of water. The girls approached cautiously.

"Nice bear," Margaret said, trying to sound confident.

"See, we've brought you something to eat," Annie added, as she carefully emptied the bag of popcorn next to the animal's water dish.

Moving from his upright position on his haunches to all fours, he snuffed at the corn. Then he ate, glancing curiously at the girls from time to time.

Poor thing, Annie thought, as she watched him eat. Tied to a chain here in Wakarusa when he could be off in the Canadian woods where the Elys found him—tiny and alone without a mother in sight. How horrible his life must be. He should be free—and so should Sandy. I'm not going to tie him up again—ever.

The girls watched the bear finish his treat and then slurp water from his dish. Neither one talked as they left the bear and walked back to the town square, above which Wakarusa's only stoplight blinked uselessly at the crowd milling below.

The band concert was over, and the girls met Bobby at the popcorn stand.

"Hey, I saw you two out of the corner of my eye trying to make me laugh," he said.

"Why didn't you look at us?" Annie asked.

"Are you kidding? Old Man Bowers would have shot me if I had missed that part. He was already mad at Amy 'cause her clarinet was squeaking." Bobby said.

Margaret interrupted. "It's almost time for the movie to start."

Joining the crowd, the three walked past stores, still filled with people, to the town park. There adults and children were sitting on wooden benches and canvas chairs brought from home. On the edges of the crowd, trying to remain invisible, were a few Amish who had dared to go against their church's decisions and participate in the pleasures of the worldly.

Suddenly, black and white figures jerked across the screen as the movie began.

"Oh boy, Tom Mix!" said Bobby. The three friends plopped down on a wooden bench in the front row and began the weekly battle with the mosquitoes as Bobby's hero rode across the screen on his white horse.

Except for thinking about Ely's bear, Annie felt good that night as she got ready for bed. While brushing her teeth, she thought of Bobby. In spite of the fact that his father was a dentist, Bobby never brushed his. When his parents were around, he'd just go in the bathroom, turn on the water, and pretend to brush. That was really kind of icky. Besides, after awhile your teeth get scummy and taste funny. She wondered if Bobby ate many apples. Annie had read somewhere that apples were "nature's toothbrush."

Back in her room, she looked at the *National Geographic* maps pasted on the walls and at the lavender and green parasols from John on her dresser. Every night, before she went to sleep, she would examine her maps and think about places she wanted to go when she grew up—Greece, England, Japan maybe, Spain. . . . Her thoughts turned again to Ely's bear. Climbing out of bed, she tiptoed down the steps and out the front door. Walking to the woodshed, she found Sandy and untied him.

Chapter Four

Decoding Secrets

July. "It's too hot to sleep upstairs tonight," Mrs. Ziegler said, as she folded a comforter in half lengthwise and made a bed for Annie on the floor in the downstairs hallway. Sleeping in front of the open door, Annie could catch whatever breeze there was.

Annie liked this change in routine, and being close to the front door made it easier to sneak in and out at night to check on Sandy. Like everyone else, he had been grumpy lately. Annie suspected he wasn't feeling well.

She lay on the comforter, her bones digging into the hard floor, and listened to her parents talk softly in bed—this seemed to be the only time they didn't argue. Soon all she heard was the whir of their fan stirring up the hot air.

She crept quietly out the front door in her nightgown. The grass felt like straw under her bare feet as she walked back to the woodshed, where she found Sandy curled up in a corner.

"Why have you been so ornery?" she asked while she petted his head. "You know you shouldn't snap at people—especially Mr. Sayers. He's already mad at you. Don't you feel well? Maybe it's the heat. It won't stay this way long."

Sandy's only response was to look up at Annie with sad eyes and wag his tail once or twice. Then he sniffed at a patch of gray fur nearby.

"What do you have?" asked Annie. Touching the object gingerly, she quickly withdrew her hand.

"Why, it's a dead rabbit!" Light from the moon, coming out from beneath a cloud, trickled down on the gray fur, and Annie saw the glint of a trap still gripping the dead animal's body.

The air was already hot and muggy the next morning when the popping of Fourth of July firecrackers awakened her. She wadded up her bed in a corner so that her parents could get in and out the front door.

She dressed quickly and, after her Wheaties and Ovaltine, went next door to her father's office. Sandy wasn't around. Annie thought he was probably checking out the Karschmans' new dog. Although the grass was brown from the drought, red roses, blue delphiniums, and some white larkspur bloomed in the garden, thanks to her father's constant watering. "Red, white, and blue," Annie said to herself. "Perfect!"

Dr. and Mrs. Ziegler sat on the leather-like chairs in her father's waiting room reading the *Chicago Tribune*. Since it was a holiday, Nora was at home—a farm south of town—helping her mother get ready for market next week. On weekends and holidays Nora baked angel food cakes, using a dozen egg whites for each cake. Then her mother and sister would take the caramel-frosted desserts to the city market in South Bend and sell them for fifty cents each.

"Morning, Annie," Dr. Ziegler said when Annie walked in the waiting room.

"Nome, Alaska, has broken a heat record with 81 degrees," said Mrs. Ziegler to Annie.

"Are there any pictures?" asked Annie, imagining Eskimos in furs standing next to a puddle of water with one square of ice—the remains of their igloo.

"No, but four people collapsed and died in South Bend yesterday because of the heat, and there is a rabies epidemic in

Elkhart. All dogs have to be tied and kept at home. That's the law." She paused and looked sternly at Annie.

"Elkhart is twelve miles away," said Annie as she headed for the door. She added, "I think I'll go to Bobby's."

Her mother seemed not to hear her as she continued to read aloud. "Penny Ice Fund for Poor Started in Indianapolis. Blocks of ice, costing three cents each are being given to. . . ." her voice trailed off.

Annie stole a glance at her father to check his reaction to the news of the rabies epidemic, but he was reading a section of the newspaper intently.

Annie crossed the street to the Myerses' house and found the front door open. She pressed her nose to the screen looking for Bobby while pushing the doorbell. Within thirty seconds he came bounding down the stairs into the front hall. His house was large and had two stairways, front and back, connecting the second floor to the first. It also had a third floor with a pool table. Annie liked the Myers family. They seemed so worldly: Cokes in the ice box, funny rugs (called Orientals) on the floor, Mrs. Myers getting her hair done every week at Grace's Beauty Shoppe. Some day, she decided, she would be like them.

Bobby invited Annie in and they went up to his room, where he had his stamp collection spread out on his bed, a table, and the floor.

Annie stepped carefully to a vacant corner.

"Can I see your Code Captain's belt?" she asked, coming straight to the point.

"Well," Bobby replied, "you can see part of it. But you can't see the secret code on the back of the buckle. You know the rules."

"But I've already sent in my Ovaltine labels. Mine will be here soon."

"I know," he said.

"So let me see the code—or at least give me a hint," Annie pleaded.

"No," Bobby said firmly. "You'll just have to wait."

Annie bit her lip. "That's mean," she said, stalking out the door and stepping on a few stamps.

"Yours will be here soon," Bobby called after her as she thumped down the steps.

"Yeah," she muttered, letting the screen door slam behind her.

Church bells awakened Annie the next morning. She stretched, her body feeling stiff. Sleeping on the floor wasn't so much fun after all.

"Almost time for church," her father said between coughs. The first thing Dr. Ziegler did when he got up was to light a cigarette on his way to the bathroom.

Annie rolled up her bed and went upstairs to wash and get dressed. She could hear her parents' voices in the kitchen below while brushing her teeth.

"Well, I'm still worried about him," Mrs. Ziegler said.

"But he's doing OK," Dr. Ziegler replied.

"What do you know—you and your predictions. He's five hundred miles away in that clinic and the doctors are probably lying about his chances."

"Now Mrs. Ziegler, I doubt that they are lying. Maybe they are just being optimistic."

"Well, I don't believe them," she said emphatically.

"Lower your voice. Annie will hear you."

"Well, it's about time she learns that other people have problems, too," Mrs. Ziegler said.

Annie stopped brushing her teeth. They must be talking about John, that world traveler and favorite relative of the family. Before Annie's mom and dad were married, Mrs.

Ziegler had taught school in a one-room schoolhouse, and Annie remembered hearing her mother say that she had used most of her salary to send John to college.

Annie thought back to her mother's telephone conversations and then to her weeping behind the closed door. She shuddered, thinking of the pictures of cancer in the medical book and of her own skirt. "I don't want any breakfast," she said as she walked into the kitchen.

"I want to continue my series of sermons on love," Reverend Crumly's voice intoned from the pulpit.

Annie looked up at the Methodist minister in his black robe. Behind him and to the left was the altar with its cross and lighted candles. On either side of the altar, divided by an aisle of purple carpeting, the choir—three men and four women—sat solemnly. All the women, except for Mrs. Crumly, fanned themselves with cardboard fans printed with the words "Moore's Funeral Home." The men tried not to look hot; like the women and Reverend Crumly, they too had on black robes. Annie could see the sweat rolling down the sides of Mr. Loucks's face into his collar, while Mr. Harrington kept brushing a fly away from his left ear.

The minister continued. "Last week, if you recall, I spoke of the necessity of the knowledge of death in order for love to exist." Apparently no one recalled, so he seemed to change his mind and stuck in a quick review of last week's sermon. Then he went on. "This week, the one in which our nation celebrates its freedom, I'd like to speak about the necessity of freedom in order for love to exist. However, I want to focus our thoughts today on personal, rather than political freedom."

Annie looked across the aisle at Mrs. Wingrab, her social studies teacher, to see her reaction to Reverend Crumly's words, but the smooth look on Mrs. Wingrab's face stayed the same. Maybe she wasn't listening.

"In order for love to exist," the minister said, "there must be a modicum of freedom. We see this in our families. Children cannot be forced to love their parents. It is only when they are older and free to choose that they can truly return the love that has been given them. This same principle holds true in regard to our Heavenly Father, who does not force us to love Him and serve Him but who gives us freedom of choice."

Annie tried to wiggle, but her bare legs stuck to the wooden pew. They made a squinching sound as she raised them one at a time. She wondered if the varnish had stuck to them and imagined herself walking out of church with her skirt sticking to the back of her newly varnished legs.

"On the other hand," Reverend Crumly said with more intensity, "we, because of evil in our hearts, may choose not to love others and to serve God; hence, we must always be aware of the possible danger inherent in our freedom to choose. In other words, we must use our freedom wisely and responsibly, for an important part of maturity is the judicious use of freedom."

Just then a fly landed on Mr. Harrington's bald head. He whacked at it, but it got away.

Annie wiggled some more and looked behind her. She saw Bobby sitting next to his older brother. He had his church bulletin rolled into a tube and was using it like a spyglass to watch Reverend Crumly and the choir members.

Finally, Mrs. Wheatly began pumping out the strains of "My Country 'tis of Thee" on the organ. The congregation stood, colors of lavender and blue with bits of red and yellow glimmering down on them from the stained-glass windows. Reverend Crumly gave the benediction, and church was over for another week.

"Northern Indiana will reach the high of mid-nine-ties with no rain in sight," stated the July 21st *Tribune*. Annie didn't care about the heat. Her Little Orphan Annie Code Captain's belt had arrived in the mail that morning.

Cranking the wall phone in the back hallway, Annie lifted the receiver and gave Margaret's number to Gladys, the operator.

"Guess what, Margaret! It came today," Annie said.

"What came?" asked Margaret, who read books rather than listening to the radio.

"My Code Captain's belt! It's red, white, and blue and has a brass buckle with the secret code printed behind it," continued Annie breathlessly.

"Well, why can't you just use your Orphan Annie badge to figure out the messages?" said Margaret, more polite than curious.

The badges, which both Bobby and Annie often wore, were brass shields about two inches high. At the top of the shield the year 1936 was embossed. On the lower part of the shield was a circle of 26 tiny openings; next to the openings were the numbers 1 through 26. Behind the shield was a movable dial on which the letters of the alphabet were printed out of order. The tiny openings served as windows through which these letters could be seen and matched to a number.

Each weekday, at the end of the fifteen-minute radio program, Pierre Andre, the announcer, would give *Orphan Annie* listeners a secret message in which clues to the next day's adventures would be hidden. Mr. Andre would begin his message with the key to decoding, such as "A=1." Then *Orphan Annie* fans all over the country would dial the back of their badges so that A appeared in the small window above 1.

On special days, however, Mr. Andre announced a super-secret message for that select group who had sent in extra Ovaltine labels for a Code Captain's belt. Only those favored people knew the secret decoding key. And now Annie was one of them.

Annie tried to explain the intricacies of the badge and decoding to Margaret, but she finally gave up. She hung up the receiver and looked at her belt, smoothing out the red, white, and blue band. Then she looked at the secret code key behind the buckle. "Z=1," she said to herself for the hundredth time that morning.

Three-thirty and time for *Jack Armstrong*. Annie sat next to the family's cathedral radio, its arched walnut cabinet contrasting with the flowered wallpaper behind it. She twisted the knobs in order to tune out the static and bring in the strains of the All-American Boy's theme song. Only fifteen minutes to go.

At 3:45 Pierre Andre's smooth voice announced the latest episode of *Little Orphan Annie*. Annie listened intently while her heroine tried to discover what was behind a series of accidents at the circus. The program ended as Orphan Annie and her friend Solly overheard the two villains talking about the trapeze artist's fall from the high wire. Then Mr. Andre informed Orphan Annie fans all over the country that today's code badge key was 1=H.

"Write down the following numbers," he said, "so that you will know in advance about tomorrow's adventures: 16, 11, space, 25, 17, 4, 11, 1, 6, space, 1, 15, 2."

During the commercial, Annie set the movable letters so that H was opposite 1 and translated the message: "We pushed him." Just as she had suspected, the trapeze artist's fall was no accident.

Then Mr. Andre read the announcement she had been waiting for. "And now *Orphan Annie* fans, I have a very special message for Little Orphan Annie Code Captains. Only you will know in advance what will happen next week. Pick up your pencils and write down the following numbers. Then use the secret Code Captain's key, which only you know, to decode this special message."

Annie copied the numbers down on the back of a used envelope. Then she set the badge at Z=1. The message she decoded was "Sandy in danger."

Thinking immediately of her own dog rather than Orphan Annie's, she ran to the back door. There Sandy lay on the steps licking his front paw. Relieved, she sat on the back steps and rubbed her dog's ears.

Chapter Five

The Graceful Brown Horse

August. Annie didn't sleep well that night on her pallet in front of the open door. Rolling over and over trying to get comfortable on her makeshift bed, she dug her knees and elbows into the hard floor underneath. The air was hot and muggy, so that she felt as if she were breathing through a wet washcloth.

When she finally fell asleep, the birds had begun their early morning chirping. She dreamt that Sandy and she were walking in a meadow, but the flowers and weeds were brown and crackly from the heat and lack of water. Then Sandy began to run ahead of her; she couldn't keep up with him. Feeling certain that something dreadful lay ahead, she called to him, "Sandy, Sandy, be careful!" But he didn't seem to hear her.

The sun was shining when she awoke. Townspeople were walking on the sidewalk in front of the Zieglers' house attending to their day's business, and she forgot about her dream.

Bobby came by later in the day. "So you got your Code Captain's belt and know the secret code now," he said.

"Yeah, no thanks to you," Annie replied.

"Well, I was just following the rules."

"Since when are you so interested in rules?" Annie asked.

Bobby decided to change the subject. "Let's see if Mr. Shroeder has any horses to shoe today."

Across the alley from Annie's father's office was Mr. Shroeder's blacksmith shop. Every weekday Amish men and other farmers would bring in their horses to be shoed or their broken buggies or farm implements to be fixed.

"Morning, Mr. Shroeder," said Bobby politely.

Both Bobby and Annie knew if they stayed out of the way, they could stand in the open doorway of the blacksmith's shop and watch him work. This morning he had to make shoes for a graceful brown horse that pulled one of the buggies parked in the alley. The sweat rolled down the smith's face as he stirred up the fire on the raised hearth near the open doorway. Annie watched him squeeze the bellows, making the coals glow. Then he took a metal horseshoe off the rack, and placing the horse's knee against his leather apron, he held the shoe to the bottom of the horse's hoof to check on the fit.

The horse's owner stood holding the animal's harness and occasionally patting its neck, while the animal stood patiently, not bothered by Mr. Shroeder's efforts. It must trust him, Annie thought. After the smith examined the metal shoe carefully, he picked it up with a pair of tongs and placed it in the burning coals. Selecting a large metal file, he went back to the horse and began filing the animal's hoof.

"Wonder if that hurts," mused Bobby.

"No," Annie replied. "Mr. Shroeder told me that a horse's hoof is like our fingernail or toenail and there's no feeling in it."

By this time the metal shoe was hot. The smith took his tongs, which were about three feet in length, and extracted the glowing shoe from the burning coals. He carried the metal to his anvil and began pounding on it with a large iron hammer. After he had beaten the horseshoe into the desired shape, he picked it up with his tongs and plunged it into the horse tank full of water.

"I like the hiss it makes when it hits the water," Bobby

42

said.

"Yeah," Annie replied absentmindedly. She was admiring the movements of the horse as it flicked its tail and twitched its skin to keep off the flies.

Mr. Shroeder pulled the cooled horseshoe from the massive water tank and, lifting up the horse's foot, tried the curved metal shoe on for size. If a shoe didn't fit, he'd fire it up and hammer it again, but today this one fit perfectly. Taking some large square-headed nails from the pockets of his leather apron and using a wooden-headed hammer, he nailed the shoe onto the horse's foot. As Mr. Shroeder was about to fit the fourth shoe, the town's fire siren began to wail. All the dogs in the neighborhood, including Sandy, joined its mournful howl. Mr. Shroeder took off his leather apron, dropped it, and ran down the alley to the town park.

From out of nowhere, cars raced to the town square, their brakes screeching as their owners parked them haphazardly at the curb. Volunteer firemen, the town's heroes, were gathering on the square. Mr. Harrington, in his white paint clothes, was the first to arrive. Then, one of Mr. Townsend's customers came running out of the barber shop next door to the smith's. He still had white lather beneath his chin, reminding Annie of Amos Frederick's dog. Mr. Cooper didn't even bother to close his car door, and Annie wondered who was taking care of the gas station. Two of the Smith brothers jumped out of their car—the third one had been riding on the running board. They must be building a house nearby.

Suddenly, Harold came running towards the volunteers as Mr. Shroeder, their chief, arrived at the town square, the siren of his truck adding to the din. The stucco building in the town park housed the town's two fire trucks—one filled with chemicals for fires in the country where there was no water supply, the other with hoses to attach to hydrants for fires in town.

The main siren, attached to the roof of the bank building, was started by Gladys, the telephone operator. Annie felt the siren's wail in every part of her body, and its vibrations made her want to cry. She felt like this when she saw someone on crutches or with a broken arm, only then just her foot or her arm hurt. Now the siren's sound echoed in her legs, her arms, and her stomach and made her feel unsettled and disconnected, like a flock of startled birds were flying off inside her in many directions.

Five minutes went by, and in that time nine men and two fire trucks had assembled at the town square. Mr. Shroeder jumped out of his truck and called Gladys from a phone, attached to the outside of the bank building just for this purpose, to find out where the fire was.

"It's at Loucks's barn," he called to the men. All but Mr. Sayers jumped onto the back of the chemical truck, donning their black fire coats and hats, while the truck roared north of town. Annie felt the vibrations diminish as the sound of its siren grew dimmer and dimmer.

Mr. Sayers, who drove the truck with the water hoses, turned right at the square and rumbled past Annie's house back to the stucco building in the park.

Gladys started the town siren again—two blasts—to let the people know that the fire was in the country.

"Whose farm is it?" Nora asked Annie when she and Bobby came running back to Dr. Ziegler's office from the town square.

"Loucks's barn," replied Bobby, while Annie caught her breath.

"Oh, no," said Nora. "They milk a lot of cows."

Annie's mother and the Karschmans were all on the sidewalk talking excitedly about the fire.

"Well, let's go see it," said Mrs. Karschman.

"Can we go, too?" Annie and Bobby asked her simultaneously.

"Yes, there's room," she said.

Annie's mother, caught up in the excitement of the event, nodded her head when Annie asked permission to go with the Karschmans.

Bobby didn't check with his mother but climbed in the back of the Karschmans' old Packard with Annie.

"You didn't ask your mother," Annie reminded him.

"Yeah, I know," Bobby said with a grin on his face, "but that would be kinda hard 'cause she's at the beauty shop. Probably under the hair dryer reading a magazine right now and doesn't even know about the fire."

For a moment Annie wished her mother went to Grace's Beauty Shoppe, too. Instead, her mother had secretly been going to see a psychiatrist in South Bend, who told Mrs. Ziegler she needed a hobby. Annie suspected that she was becoming her mother's "hobby," and the thought made her bite her lip. Yet her mother seemed less tense, and her parents didn't argue so much either.

Mrs. Karschman wheeled the Packard around and headed north of town. So far as Annie knew, there wasn't another car like the Karschmans' in all of Wakarusa. For one thing, it must have been the longest car in town: it had a front seat, a back seat, and fold-down seats between the front and back. Annie and Bobby sat on these pop-up seats now gliding along like royalty between the roadside rows of wild orange tiger lilies and Queen Anne's lace.

Sitting in the front seat with Mrs. Karschman was her married daughter, Imogene, who was visiting her mother that day to help her can tomatoes. (The Karschmans canned all their own fruits and vegetables and made their own laundry soap.) In the back seat were Mrs. Karschman's two younger daughters, Maryanne and Beatrice, and their cousin, Jane. Irene, Mrs. Karschman's other daughter, was working at the bank, which didn't even close for fires. The group talked excitedly as they, along with many other townspeople, sped toward the fire.

Within a few minutes they were outside the city limits, sailing like the wind past the sign whose reverse side said, "Welcome to Wakarusa, population 998." Small farms, each with its own house, barn, and assorted outbuildings, lined the narrow road. All were neat and well kept except for the old Erskine place. Bramble bushes and honeysuckle vines covered the grounds of the once spacious house whose vacant windows stared out onto the road.

Suddenly, ahead and to their right, a pillar of black smoke rose in the sky. Then they saw the red-orange flames licking away at the walls of the barn.

"The animals, the animals," cried Annie.

"It's OK," Imogene said from the front seat. "Look in the fields—you can see Mr. Loucks's neighbors—they've got them."

Annie turned and saw a number of farmers, each with a cow or two on a rope leading nervous animals around in circles. To the side was a farmer trying to quiet two horses. One of them reminded Annie of the graceful animal Mr. Shroeder had been shoeing. Then, without warning, the brown horse broke away and headed into the flaming barn.

Above the noise of the crackling fire and the yelling men, Annie heard a loud piercing scream.

It was her own.

Mrs. Karschman stopped the car. "I wish we hadn't come," she said. Both Maryanne and Beatrice were crying, and Bobby had a strange look on his face.

One of the firemen yelled, "Get back!" At that moment the roof of the barn collapsed, bringing down the flaming walls and crushing everything inside.

That evening after dinner Annie and her father sat on the back porch steps. Sandy lay at Annie's feet. In the sky to the north, traces of smoke could still be seen.

"Why did that horse run back in the barn?" she asked her father.

"Because that was its home—the only safe place it knew," he said.

"But it was burning."

"Yes, the horse panicked," her father said.

"But it could have run away," Annie said.

"The horse made the wrong choice—we all do sometimes, Annie," her father said gently.

The heat continued, twenty-six days without rain. Many farmers lost their corn crop, including the Loucks, whose neighbors were helping them build a new barn. Annie and Sandy walked listlessly down the alley to the park. Margaret was going to give Annie a lesson in swearing that afternoon.

Bobby and Margaret were sitting on the swings when they arrived. It was so hot even Margaret was barefoot, making a pattern in the sand beneath the swing with her big toe. Bobby was twisting his swing around and around, then letting it whirl back to its original position, surely making himself dizzy. Margaret was the first to speak. "I wish August was over and it was the first week in September. I'm tired of vacation."

Annie didn't want to admit it, but she was getting tired of vacation, too. By now, even Nora was grouchy, horning in to demand of her: "Make your bed, clean your room, do the dishes." If her dad started, it wouldn't take an Orphan Annie Code Badge to figure out that vacation was over. But she didn't say any of these things. Instead she just repeated, like the chorus of an old song, "I hate school and all those dumb rules."

"Yeah," said Bobby without conviction.

"But rules are necessary," replied Margaret.

Both Annie and Bobby looked at her in surprise.

"Well, at least some rules," said Margaret.

"Such as?" said Bobby.

"Well, I think health rules are important."

"Like brushing your teeth," sneered Bobby.

"Not really," said Margaret, "I was thinking of those sparrows they brought to school assembly last spring."

"You mean the ones that creepy man with the mustache brought in cages and then used that machine to force cigarette smoke into them and then they all keeled over dead after smoking two cigarettes?" Bobby said all in one breath.

"Yeah, that's the one," Margaret answered.

Annie felt creepy inside herself, remembering the chirping sparrows falling silently to the floor of their cage.

"I think if cigarettes are going to kill those sparrows, they're probably bad for people. Safety rules are important, too," continued Margaret.

Annie bit her lip as she thought of her father smoking two packs of cigarettes a day and sometimes failing to stop at stop signs. "Hey, Margaret, what about those swear words you promised to teach us?"

The three friends sat down on some withered grass under a tree while Sandy wandered off.

"Well," Margaret replied. "I talked to my brother, and he said that when you're mad you say 'Damn,' and when you're really mad—"

"Huh," Bobby interrupted, "I could have told you that."

"But wait," Margaret said patiently. "There's more."

At that moment they heard a cracking sound, like the rifle shots in the Tom Mix movies. Then came the startled cry of a dog.

❧ Welcome ❧
to
Wakarusa

Population: 998

Chapter Six

Sandy

After searching the park, Annie and her two friends found Sandy lying on the mat in front of her father's office door.

Near the dog's head was a splotch of blood. Sandy's eyes were closed. Annie got down on her knees and touched the animal gently—she was afraid to move him. "Oh, Sandy," she crooned over and over. Once Sandy opened his eyes, but they fluttered shut again.

"What happened?" Dr. Ziegler asked from the other side of the screen door.

"Sandy was shot while we were in the park," Bobby said.

Margaret, whose face was very pale, stood speechless.

Dr. Ziegler carefully opened the door to avoid bumping Sandy's body. Then he knelt down and examined the dog's bleeding head. "Yes, the bullet went in here," he said to himself.

"Annie, we need to take Sandy to Dr. Smith's and have him remove the bullet. You get in the car, and I'll put Sandy in your lap. It won't hurt him to ride three blocks. Dr. Smith is a good vet," he continued reassuringly.

Annie did as her father suggested. Nora must have called ahead, for Dr. Smith and his assistant, Phil Stone, came out to the parking lot and met Annie and her father as they drove in. Phil eased the unconscious animal from Annie's lap.

Annie watched as a few drops of blood fell to the ground from the dog's wound. Oh, Sandy! Oh, Sandy! Over and over the words went in her head as she watched Phil gently carry her dog towards Dr. Smith's office.

Back home, Annie went to her room, pulled down the window shades, and shut the door. She was lying on her bed, face buried in her pillow, when she heard a knock. She didn't answer. Then her mother's voice said, "Annie, may I come in?"

"What do you want?" Annie said through the pillow.

Her mother opened the door and came into the darkened room. She sat on the edge of the bed and put her hand on Annie's shoulder.

"I'm sorry, Annie," she said.

"Why? You didn't shoot him."

"I know. I'm just sorry it happened." Mrs. Ziegler rubbed her daughter's tense shoulders as she spoke.

Silence. Then Mrs. Ziegler said, "You must have seen that I have been worried about your cousin John."

"Yes," said Annie softly.

"Well, I've had good news about him. He's had cancer, and I was afraid he would die, but the doctors in Minnesota operated on him last week and he's doing very well. Perhaps Dr. Smith can operate on Sandy and save his life. I hope so."

That last sentence surprised Annie. Maybe her mother wasn't so bad after all. Mrs. Ziegler squeezed Annie's shoulder and left the room, carefully closing the door behind her.

"I hope so, too," said Annie, burying her face in her pillow and feeling very much alone.

Annie sensed the sounds of the phone ringing downstairs. She felt sick as she heard her father's heavy footsteps ascending the stairs.

Dr. Ziegler opened the door to her room and slowly walked across to the bed. Annie could hear his uneven breathing as he sat down next to her. "Annie, your dog is dead. Dr. Smith did all he could. . . ."

Annie jumped off the bed and ran to the bathroom. She could hardly breathe. Leaning over the toilet, she began to vomit.

Chapter Seven

Revenge

That night in her room, Annie went over the day's events again and again in her mind, relentlessly checking the steps leading up to Sandy's death. Who would want to hurt Sandy? Some people were angry with him—such as those who rode bicycles past the Ziegler house. But who was mean enough to kill him? And who owned a rifle? Lots of people in Wakarusa went hunting. She had no good answers.

Outside the wind blew, making the muslin curtains quiver back and forth. Then it began to rain. For the first time in weeks, Annie felt cold. She shivered and got under the bed covers. Who shot Sandy? It was the kind of question Pierre Andre asked at the end of *Little Orphan Annie*. But she needed more than a Code Badge to figure out the answer.

Whoever did it—damn you, damn you! Annie thought.

Eventually, the rain stopped and the day's light began to seep into her room, dimly illuminating the maps on the walls. She looked at the paper parasols on her dresser, then they became a blur as tears finally came.

Annie slept. She dreamed that she was in church sitting in the front pew, but no one was sitting around her—no churchgoers, no choir, no organist—only Reverend Crumly, dressed in his black robe, high in the pulpit. He was shaking his finger at her. At first she couldn't hear his words, then his voice said, "It's you, it's you."

"What do you mean?" Annie asked from her seat.

"It's you who is responsible."

"Responsible?"

"Yes. It's you who let your dog run free."

Annie moaned in her sleep.

"But I love him," she replied.

"Did you love him enough?" the minister demanded.

"I don't know. I don't know."

The next morning was chilly, so Annie put a sweater on over her dress. She looked in the mirror while brushing her hair and saw her eyes were puffy. Who cares, she said to the mirror. She went downstairs and fixed herself the usual breakfast of Wheaties and Ovaltine. As she picked at her food, she kept thinking about Reverend Crumly. She didn't like him, but she couldn't think why. She did not remember her dream.

Her father's flowers, now brown and lifeless stalks, stood like silent sentinels in the garden; beneath them the grass was still parched in spite of last night's rain. To the side was a little mound of dirt—Sandy's grave. Annie quickly looked away. She opened the back door of her father's office and went into the side room where Nora sat at her father's desk.

Struggling to her feet, Nora silently walked over to Annie and put her arms around her. Annie bit her lip and tried not to cry. She hated having anyone see her weep, but a few tears rolled down her cheeks in spite of her efforts. Her stomach felt like the palm of old Mr. Goldberg's hand.

"Your mother is visiting your Aunt Martha, and your father is out making calls," Nora said. Annie's insides churned, and she wondered how Nora could be so calm. And Nora seemed to like everyone—even bugs. "Cute as a bug's ear." Oh, Sandy, she thought, as she felt the tears well up again.

Nora looked at Annie for a moment, then she said, "How about getting the mail for me?"

Annie shrugged her shoulders. "Might as well."

There were no mailmen in Wakarusa, only a postmistress, Flossie Peters, who ran the post office—sorting the mail, putting the mail in the proper cubbyholes, and selling stamps. Annie had memorized the combination to the Zieglers' post office box years ago and often picked up the mail that was placed there twice a day.

The air was bright and clear as she started down the street. The cicadas, announcing the coming of fall, had not yet begun their daily sawing.

"Morning, Annie," said Mr. Shroeder from the door of his blacksmith shop. "Beautiful day, isn't it?"

Annie just looked at the smith. Did he do it? Probably not, he liked animals.

She passed by Mr. Townsend's barbershop. Inside, she could see the barber putting hot towels on a customer's face. Her father went there often for a shave and sometimes a haircut. Could Mr. Townsend be the one?

Listlessly, she walked on.

"Mornin'," said Mr. Sayers curtly, walking towards the barber shop.

Annie just stared at the wizened man, remembering the scene with Frederick's dog and then the one in the park. "And take that mutt with you," he had said. "There's a law against animals running loose in this town!" He sure doesn't like animals, she thought. He doesn't even like people. She set her jaw. I bet he's the one.

When she came to the corner, she almost bumped into Tom Braden. They each glared at the other and went on.

On the square the bandstand was being set up for the last concert before school began. Morning shoppers were going in and out of Goldberg's and Keever's. Just like always. What an ugly town, she thought.

Bobby and Margaret came by that afternoon. Bobby had brushed his hair, washed his face, and tucked in his shirt. Margaret, in a pale green dress with smocking, looked the same as she usually did—neat and clean. But there was a frown above her nose that Annie had never noticed before.

"We're sorry about Sandy," Bobby began.

"Yes," Margaret added.

Annie had no words. Biting her lip and squinting, she nodded. Then she said, "Let's talk about something else."

"Who do you think did it?" asked Bobby, unable to stop himself.

Margaret looked startled, and the frown deepened.

"I don't know," said Annie.

"Well, how can we find out?" he asked.

Before Annie could answer, Bobby continued. "Now, the Shadow would go about finding the killer by hunting for clues and questioning people."

The Shadow, whose real name was Lamont Cranston, was the hero of another of the radio programs that Bobby and Annie loved to listen to. Unlike *Jack Armstrong* and *Little Orphan Annie*, the show was broadcast on Sunday afternoons and lasted half an hour. A friend of Bobby's, Roger Riesenberger, liked this program so much that when his parents asked him to pick a name for his new baby brother, he chose the Shadow's name. In time, however, Lamont Cranston Riesenberger came to be known as Monty.

Annie always smiled when she thought of Monty and how he got his name. She started to smile today, then stopped.

Bobby continued energetically. "I haven't interviewed anyone, but I did look for clues." He reached in his knickers and pulled out a spent rifle shell. "I found this in the vacant lot across the street from the park."

Margaret put her hand to her mouth, and Annie looked with horror at the empty shell.

Bobby looked at the faces of the two girls and then down at his extended hand with the shell in it. "I think I'd better go now," he said, embarrassed about the girls' reaction to seeing the shell.

"Wait a minute, I've got an idea," said Annie.

"May I help you?" Harold said, looking over the meat case at Annie, Bobby, and Margaret.

"I want to report a murder," said Annie.

Harold's eyes opened wide. "Whose murder?"

"Sandy's. And I want you to arrest the killer."

"Well, I can't very well do that unless I have some evidence," said Harold.

"We do have evidence. Here," said Bobby, holding the shell in his outstretched hand.

"Well, kids," said Harold gravely, "we better talk this over. Let's go in my office."

Harold led the way into a crowded cubbyhole at the back of the store filled with stacked boxes, an old roll-top desk covered with papers, and three folding chairs. A single light bulb, dangling at the end of a cord, shone down on Annie and her friends as they seated themselves across from Harold, who sat at the desk.

"Now, then," said Harold, "tell me what happened."

In a quavering voice Annie told the story of her dog's shooting while Bobby fidgeted with the shell and Margaret's eyes filled with tears.

After she had finished, Harold sat silently thinking. Then he spoke. "I'm really sorry about your dog, Annie," he began, "but I'm afraid there's not much I can do about it. You see, it's not as if Sandy was human and I could go about issuing search warrants in order to look for guns and such. It's just not that way." Pausing to clear his throat, he added, "Besides, Sandy really should not have been running loose in the park. You remember after Frederick's dog got rabies, the town council passed a law about dogs running loose."

Annie bit her lip and looked hard at Harold. "Then you're not going to do anything?"

"I'm afraid I can't, Annie," he said.

Seated on the swings in the park, the three friends discussed Harold's decision.

"It's not fair," said Annie. "What good are laws if they don't help kids and dogs?"

"Yeah," said Bobby, "kids always get the raw end of the deal."

Margaret didn't say anything.

"If it was Little Orphan Annie's dog that had been shot, I bet the killer would have been punished by now," said Annie. "After all, killing's a lot worse than breaking some dumb town ordinance."

"Yeah," said Bobby, "I bet Daddy Warbucks would've had Punjab string the killer up by his thumbs or boil him in oil."

"But I'm not Little Orphan Annie and the killer isn't going to be caught and punished and life isn't fair," said Annie. "It's not like Z=1 and everything comes out even. It's just not fair my dog should be killed for breaking a dumb ordinance."

Margaret and Bobby both nodded in agreement.

"Look," said Bobby suddenly, "there goes Old Man Sayers down the alley. Do you think he did it?"

"I don't know," Annie said. "But if he can break the law and get away with it, I can, too."

"Well, I see your favorite person is going to be at the state fair soon," Mrs. Ziegler said to her husband that evening at dinner.

"Yes, I read in the *Tribune* that President Roosevelt is

coming to speak about the drought."

"Just like a politician, making a speech about the drought after we've had rain. What can he do? Besides he's going to lose to Landon this November."

"I don't think so," Dr. Ziegler said, his voice rising.

Back to normal, Annie thought, at least for them.

That night Annie went to her bedroom and pretended to get ready for bed. She listened carefully, and after she thought her parents were asleep, she tiptoed down the steps and out the front door, which the Zieglers, like most of the people in town, never locked.

The full moon shone down on the empty street, coloring it silvery gray. No lights were on at Bobby's or at the Karschmans' house. Annie shivered—from the cold and fear—as she crossed the street and cautiously walked down the alley past Goldbergs' and Keevers' back doors on one side and the Karschmans' garden on the other.

White stalks of Mrs. Karschman's blooming nicotiana shone in the moonlight; Annie sniffed the air in vain for its sweet scent. Under her feet the soft crunch of stones made the night's only sound. As she approached the park, the moonlit shadows of the Karschmans' barn darkened her path. She trembled while walking through the tunneled shadow into the weed-filled lot opposite the park. At the far end of the lot was the back door to Mr. Sayers's repair shop, where during the day he fixed people's broken irons, toasters, or lamps. Tonight it was dark and deserted.

Annie walked up to the back door of the wood-frame building, reached into the pocket of her pinafore, and pulled out a small piece of cardboard. On it was printed

I know you did it.
15-3-3-8-4

Using some white cloth tape from her father's office, she attached the sign to the back door. Earlier, she had set her Orphan Annie Code Badge to Z=1 in order to arrive at 15-3-3-8-4—her first name. At least her note wasn't completely anonymous. Her father always said that people who didn't sign their names to letters were cowards.

As she turned to leave, she looked across the alley to the pile of sand where Sandy had been digging not long before he was shot. Then, almost without thinking, she bent over until she spotted a good-sized rock. Picking it up, she turned and hurled it through the windowpane to the right of Mr. Sayers's shop door.

The sound of shattering glass and the clunk of the rock as it landed on the floor broke the night's stillness. Annie turned and ran as fast as she could down the alley to the front steps of her house. There she stopped and caught her breath before carefully opening the front door and tiptoeing up the steps to her room.

That night Reverend Crumly's face appeared again in her dream. "It's not my fault," she cried out to him. In the morning, she felt uneasy as she dressed for the first day of school. She didn't know why, but her insides fluttered again like a flock of startled birds, as if she were hearing the warning wail of the town's fire siren.

Chapter Eight

Life is Not Fair

September. "Annie, you're limping," said Bobby as they walked to the town square to meet Margaret.

"Yeah, my shoes are too small," said Annie with a grumpy look on her face. That morning she had refused to put on the new orthopedic shoes her mother had bought her—ones that were supposed to keep her toes from turning in—and she was remembering her parting comment to her mother: "I'm not going to wear clunky shoes like you!" Annie thought she'd seen her mother's eyes fill with tears, but Mrs. Ziegler had turned away quickly, and Annie went out the door without saying good-bye.

Now she limped painfully in last spring's scuffed brown oxfords to the square, where Margaret waited for them in a pale pink dress and shiny brown shoes.

"Hey, Margaret, guess what I got," said Bobby. "A Ford coil!"

"A what?" asked Margaret.

"A Ford coil. Actually, two of them."

"So what are they for?"

"They're about the size of a baby's shoe box, and they're from old cars. They can be used for sending messages."

"Hey, that sounds OK," said Annie. "Can I have one of them?"

"Yeah," said Bobby. "The only problem is it's against the law to use them because they interfere with people's radio programs."

"You mean they make static?" asked Margaret.

"Not exactly. Each time you press the attached key, it makes a buzz sorta like Morse code, and people's radios pick up each buzz," said Bobby.

"We could make up and send messages back and forth using our Orphan Annie Code Badges," said Annie, forgetting her grumpiness. "Why don't I pick it up after school?"

"OK," said Bobby. "Just don't tell your folks."

By this time the three had walked past Ely's Farm Implement Store and the post where the bear was tied. At least it will be free again when the Elys take it to Canada next week, Annie told herself. She wished she was going with it.

Instead, she stood in front of the Wakarusa Community School with its two matching entrances—one marked GRADE over the doorway and the other marked HIGH—separated by the windows of Mrs. Crumly's first-grade room and an enormous bed of orange and yellow marigolds.

Grades one through six began the day by meeting for fall assembly in the desk-filled room facing the stage. Normally, the room served as the junior and senior high study hall and library. Annie and her friends sat as far back in the room as possible. There they overheard Mrs. Wingrab, the social studies teacher, say, "It's as if those little kids had poison ivy or something. None of the older students will sit near them."

"Yes, I think the older kids are afraid that sitting near first graders will make them seem less grown up," replied Mrs. Diller, the music teacher.

Mr. Moore, the bald principal, whom all the big kids called Sparkle Dome behind his back, blew into the microphone, then tapped his finger against it. "Testing, testing. Can you hear me?" he asked.

"Well, at least that creepy man with the sparrows isn't here," said Annie to Margaret.

"You mean the one who kills them with cigarette smoke?" asked Margaret.

"Shhh," came the voice of one of the teachers standing behind them.

"Let us begin with the Pledge of Allegiance and then remain standing for the invocation given today by Reverend Crumly," said Mr. Moore.

"I pledge allegiance to the flag of the United States of America," the treble voices spoke as one.

Then the baritone voice of Reverend Crumly intoned, "Our Father, as we begin this school year, let us remember our responsibilities to Thee and to others. Let us use our freedom wisely, remembering that we cannot break the laws of the universe without endangering our souls and our bodies. Amen."

Annie moved restlessly in her seat during Reverend Crumly's prayer. I can't figure out why I don't like that man, she muttered to herself.

Music class was worse than last year. Mrs. Diller, who dyed her hair and made the mistake of telling her students about it, stood at the front of the room drawing a music staff on the board with the big staff liner, which held five pieces of chalk. While she drew the treble clef, Dan Ramshaw was able to flick off four spitballs, one of which splatted onto the wall above the chalkboard. A good trick. Either Dan was getting faster or Mrs. Diller was getting slower.

"Now class, if I were to place a quarter note on the second line of the staff, what note would it be?" asked Mrs. Diller.

"Who cares?" said Steve Yoder under his breath.

"Do you know, Annie?" asked Mrs. Diller brightly.

"No," replied Annie, who had been taking piano lessons for five years. She didn't care, either.

Margaret, whose seat was behind Annie's, nudged her in the back. When Mrs. Diller wasn't looking, she handed

Annie a torn piece of cardboard from the back of someone's tablet. It said:

> *PASS THIS ON*
> *Look at Mrs. Diller*
> *Her slip is showing!*

Annie was getting ready to punch Amy Shroeder in front of her when Mrs. Diller looked up.

"What do you have, Annie?" she asked.

Annie hesitated. She didn't feel good when she lied, and she'd told Mrs. Diller one lie already that day. "Just a piece of cardboard," she answered.

"Give it here," Mrs. Diller said, smiling her Pepsodent smile that used just her mouth, not her eyes.

"No," replied Annie.

The smile disappeared. "I will see you in my office tonight immediately after school."

So what? Annie thought grimly. But that afternoon she served her time in Mrs. Diller's office, which made her miss *Jack Armstrong* and *Little Orphan Annie*.

After Mrs. Diller dismissed her, she hurried home and made a lot of quick phone calls. Thirty minutes later she was back at school having rounded up six of her friends. (Margaret wouldn't come, but Bobby was part of the group.) Together they all stood beneath Mrs. Diller's windows and sang "The old gray mare, she ain't what she used to be." When the music teacher's angry face appeared at one of the windows, they all ran, but it was too late. She had seen them.

After dinner that evening, Dr. Ziegler invited Annie to make a house call with him.

"I'll go if I don't have to do dishes," said Annie.

Mrs. Ziegler frowned, but before she could say anything, Dr. Ziegler said, "OK, you can help your mother tomorrow night," and gave Mrs. Ziegler a nod.

Annie's mother didn't reply, but turned and went in the kitchen.

Well, I will help her tomorrow night, Annie thought, as they drove past the fields of corn stacked in teepee-like shocks.

"I'm glad the farmers were able to save some of their crop," Dr. Ziegler said, slowing down but not stopping at the stop sign.

Annie half listened while thinking of Mr. Loucks's horse and of Sandy. She wished like anything that the graceful brown horse was grazing in the field and that Sandy was in the car with them now.

Several years ago, when Annie had first started riding with her father to make house calls, she'd imagined that they would see beautiful houses with wall-to-wall carpeting and sleek kitchen appliances like the ones in her mother's *Good Housekeeping* magazines. Now she knew better, for Dr. Ziegler's patients were usually poor, and their homes had linoleum on the floors and kitchen sinks with a pump rather than a faucet. Out in back, a small shack with bad smelling pits would be their only bathroom.

Yet the people they were calling on tonight seemed poorer than most of Dr. Ziegler's patients. As they drove up the lane, Annie noticed the rotting barn. Even if the farmhouses needed paint and repairs, most farms had good barns. To the side of it was a dilapidated house. In the growing darkness, Annie saw a pale yellow light coming from two of the downstairs windows. They didn't even have electricity.

An unshaven old man with bent shoulders met them at the back door.

"Hello, Doc. Glad you could come. The girl's not doin' well, and the missus is gittin' poorly, too." He opened the door so they could step inside.

A peculiar smell of age and decay was in the air. Annie tried not to breathe too deeply. They followed the man through the dimly lit kitchen, with its pump and wood-burning stove, to the room beyond. There Annie saw something she had never seen before and hoped she would never see again.

Sitting in a rocker was an old woman. On her lap was a grown person, her legs dangling over the side of the chair, her head and shoulders overlapping the other side. The scene, lit by the golden flickering of the kerosene lamps, reminded Annie of a picture she had once seen of a marble statue carved by a man named Michelangelo. It was supposed to be Mary holding the body of Jesus, her son.

What's going on here? Annie wondered, afraid to speak, especially since no one seemed to notice she was there.

The girl—really a grown woman—was crying softly while the old woman rocked and murmured to her.

"She's quieted down a lot since I called you," the old man said, "but I was afraid we couldn't git any sleep agin tonight. It's hard on the missus, you know."

"Yes, I know," said Annie's father, taking his stethoscope out of his black bag.

While her father examined the girl and then the mother, Annie waited in a darkened corner of the room. Dr. Ziegler talked to the girl for some time and then he helped the old man put her to bed. "I'll check on her again in the morning," Annie's father said as he picked up his black bag and motioned his daughter to the door.

Once they were in the car, Annie's curiosity about what she had just seen erased sadness and anger from her mind. "What's going on there? What's wrong with that girl?" she asked her father.

Dr. Zeigler paused to light a cigarette before starting

the car and his explanation. "Well, Mr. and Mrs. Sampson's daughter, Emily, has a very bad cold, and when she lies down, she can't breathe. Because she's retarded, she doesn't understand that the cold will go away soon. Instead, she thinks that when she lies down she will die."

"But how long has she been retarded?" asked Annie.

"She was born that way seventeen years ago," said Dr. Ziegler.

"Why? What caused it?"

"We don't know," replied her father. "I delivered Emily. It was a normal delivery without complications. No reason to think that she would be different from anyone else."

"Then why is she different?"

Dr. Ziegler inhaled deeply. "Well, when a baby is conceived, that is, when the father's sperm connects with the egg from the mother's womb, there are all sorts of probable combinations. That's why no two people—even identical twins— are exactly alike." Dr. Ziegler paused. "In a sense, these materials—the sperm and the egg and the genes they contain—are free to make a number of combinations. However, their freedom is limited. If two horses mate, they won't have a human baby and vice versa, but within limitations there is freedom, so perhaps even genes make mistakes."

Annie nodded her head even though she didn't quite understand.

"In a way this is what happens when a person gets cancer. The cells in the body are free to do a number of things within limitations, and they sometimes make a mistake."

"But it's not fair that some people are born retarded like Emily and that some people like John get cancer," Annie said.

"Yes, you're right, Annie," her father said sadly as he lit another cigarette. "Life is not fair."

But, thought Annie, there are some things that people

can change. She longed to tell her father about the cigarettes and the dead sparrows.

When they arrived home, Mrs. Ziegler met them at the front door, a stern look on her face. "The school principal called. What's this about you and the music teacher?"

Her mother's lecture about respect for adults—especially parents and teachers—was one Annie had heard before, so part of her mind listened and part of it planned her next move with Mr. Sayers.

When her mother finished, saying that she and Dr. Zeigler would decide on Annie's punishment in the morning, Annie limped up the steps to her bedroom. She had already made another sign and was anxious to put it up. This time, she decided, she would tape it to the front door of Mr. Sayers's house.

Even though she couldn't concentrate, she lay on her bed, fully dressed, trying to read one of her father's magazines. An article in it told about Jews in Germany who were being put in prison by a man named Hitler, not because they did anything wrong, but just because they were Jewish. Annie was glad Mr. Goldberg and his family were safe in Wakarusa.

Finally, all was quiet downstairs; Annie decided her parents were asleep. She carefully left her room and crept down the steps. A thumping noise startled her until she realized it was her own heart pounding.

All the lights but one were out in their neighbors' homes. Bobby's bedroom window just across the street had a dim light that varied in intensity, probably Bobby in bed reading with a flashlight. For a moment Annie considered crossing the street, throwing pebbles at Bobby's window screen, and asking him to go with her. Then she decided it would be too risky. It was bad enough sneaking out of the house without alarming her parents, but to take the chance of awakening

Bobby's parents—or even his brother—would be dumb. For a second the thought entered her mind that her entire campaign against Mr. Sayers was dumb, but she quickly turned that thought aside and started down the alley to his house on the far side of the town park.

She had to pick her way carefully past the back of Goldbergs' and Keevers', for the moon behind a cloud barely illuminated Mrs. Karschman's garden, much less the gray stones at Annie's feet. Annie pulled her sweater tightly around her shoulders as she passed the Karschmans' barn and the place where she thought Sandy had been shot. To her right was Mr. Sayers's appliance shop and the new window he had carefully installed. She shivered and wished she were safe and warm, home in bed, yet the sound of a dog howling in the distance brought her back to her purpose. She continued resolutely towards Mr. Sayers's house and his front door.

Cautiously approaching the front porch of the white frame house, she noticed a wooden swing suspended from the porch ceiling creaking softly back and forth in the breeze. It was hard for Annie to imagine Mr. Sayers with his beard and mean squinty eyes taking time to sit on a swing, but then it was hard to imagine Mr. Sayers living in this quaint little house. Fancy scrollwork edged the top of the porch like a fringe hanging down towards the newly painted porch railing below. Someone had skillfully added a board to make the railing alongside the swing wider. Red geraniums stood upright there like toy soldiers, while around their base white petunias trailed down the sides of orange clay pots.

Annie reached into her pocket for the sign and her father's tape. She attached it carefully to the window of the front door, framed with frost-like etching. In the emerging moonlight she read

Animal Killer!
15-3-3-8-4

As she turned to leave, she looked above her sign and through the window to a faint light coming from the back of the house. Her curiosity overcame her fear, and she sneaked around the house to where the light shone through an open window. She heard the murmur of voices. Suddenly she stumbled and fell to the ground. She had tripped over a brick, one of many enclosing a flower garden, and had landed on a row of mums. Annie lay silently, trembling a little as she heard the voices stop and then continue. Still curious, she crawled to the window and stole a quick look inside. There in the dim light was an elderly woman sitting up in bed, her white hair and sloping shoulders framed with pillows. Beside her on the edge of the bed sat old Mr. Sayers holding a bowl in one hand and a spoon in the other. He seemed to be feeding the woman some liquid from the bowl.

Annie ducked her head and sat leaning against the white boards beneath the window. For a moment she felt ashamed—ashamed for sneaking out of her house at night, for peeping into other people's windows, and for leaving mean signs on Mr. Sayers's doors. She looked at the garden where she had tripped and fallen, breaking off the stems of the mum plants, and she thought of her father's garden and the little mound of dirt in it—Sandy's grave. "If he can break the law, I can, too," she muttered to herself as she edged away from the lighted window and started home.

The sound of approaching voices persuaded her to duck into the bushes in front of Mr. Sayers's house. Peering through the branches, she saw Tom Braden and his brother. Slung over Tom's shoulder was a dead rabbit.

Chapter Nine

More Trouble

October. Annie never used the back door of her house anymore because it would force her to walk past her father's garden and the little mound of dirt there, now partially covered with falling leaves. Instead, she ran out the front door, hurrying to catch up with Bobby and Margaret on their way to school.

The air was crisp with the coming of fall, and the leaves' reds, yellows, and oranges, accented with touches of green, reflected the gold of the morning light. When Bobby saw Annie, he pretended to smoke a cigarette, blowing his steaming breath in the air. "Got your message," he said.

"Yeah, well, why didn't you send an answer?" Annie asked.

"Well," Bobby began uneasily, "my parents were listening to Jack Benny on the radio, and they were pretty mad about the noise. My dad even called someone to complain."

"So did mine," said Margaret.

"Why don't we just forget about this message stuff? I'll come by after school and pick up my Ford coil," said Bobby.

"No," said Annie firmly.

"But it's against the law to use it," said Margaret.

"So what?" replied Annie. "If old Mr. Sayers can break the law, I can, too."

"You're always saying that. But you don't know that it was Old Man Sayers who shot Sandy," Bobby began.

Annie glared at the two of them in reply.

By this time they were standing outside the GRADE entrance waiting for the bell to ring. Deciding to change the subject, Bobby said, "Annie, what are you going to be for Halloween?"

Annie paused. "I think I'll be a witch." She was making a secret list of people's windows she planned to soap, and she didn't want her friends to know about it.

"Does your mother have any empty spools of thread?" asked Margaret.

"Yeah, I think so," said Annie. "Do you want them for noise makers?"

"Oh boy! I almost forgot. Save one for me, too," Bobby said.

Each Halloween Annie and her friends would use a pocket knife to notch the edges of a large wooden spool. Then they would wrap a foot or so of string around the spool and put a large nail through the hole in its center. When they held the notched edges of the spool against a windowpane and pulled the string, it made a deafening noise.

"I think my parents are going to let me have a Halloween party in the basement," said Bobby. "I got a bunch of boxes from Mr. Goldberg, and I'm building a tunnel at the bottom of the steps that you'll have to crawl through to get to the party."

"Gee, that's great!" Margaret said.

Annie didn't say anything. She hated tight dark spaces and wasn't looking forward to climbing through Bobby's tunnel. Besides, she didn't feel like going to a party.

The furor over the music teacher episode had barely died down, yet today Annie had another idea during sixth-grade recess. The afternoon sun had warmed the October air and made the metal slide on the playground comfortable again. Next door to the school, Mrs. Schrock's mums, bright blobs of color, formed a backdrop for the angular slides and swings, whose frantic users were going up and down and back and forth, trying to cram as much activity as possible into fifteen minutes. Annie was bored with this grade-school stuff and longed to be inside with Mr. Warman's junior-high class. She could see them through the windows looking grown up and attentive while Mr. Warman paused for a moment to open a window.

I've got to move fast, she thought. Getting together six of her classmates, she explained her idea. Margaret was off reading somewhere, but Bobby joined the group, at least until he heard Annie's suggestion.

"Nope," he replied. "I got in enough trouble with Sparkle Dome the last time."

Bobby's defection and that of Amy Shroeder, who claimed she had to go to the bathroom, brought the group down to five, but even they were strong enough vocally to capture the seventh graders' attention.

"Oh, say can you see any bedbugs on me. If you can, pick a few for the red, white, and blue," they sang to the tune of the "The Star-Spangled Banner."

"Disrespectful and unpatriotic," snorted Mr. Warman as he stamped out of the room to the principal's office.

Once again, Mr. Moore called Annie's parents. This time Dr. Ziegler took over.

"Annie," he asked that evening when the two of them sat in the living room after dinner and dishes, "What's going on with you? Why are you acting this way?"

"I don't know," replied Annie, looking confused but with resentment in her voice.

"But you do know you can't continue to act this way at school, don't you?"

"But it's not my fault," said Annie, tears coming into her eyes.

"What's not your fault, Annie?" her father asked.

"It's not my fault that Sandy was shot," she blurted out.

"But who said it was your fault?"

For a moment Annie wanted to answer "Reverend Crumly," but that didn't make any sense. "I guess," she said slowly, "I think it partly my fault. In a way I killed Sandy by letting him run loose."

Dr. Ziegler looked at Annie thoughtfully and then lit a cigarette. "Well, Annie, it's true that more things can happen to an animal that's not tied. Yet a lot of dogs and cats roam around Wakarusa and the nearby countryside and nothing happens to them." He paused to inhale. "Do you remember Ely's bear? I suppose it is much happier since they took it back to Canada last month and set it free, yet it may live a shorter life than it might have, chained to a stake in Wakarusa."

"What I'm saying," he continued, "is that with freedom comes unpredictability. You couldn't see into the future, so you had no way of knowing that someone would use his freedom irresponsibly and shoot your dog. Life doesn't always add up, does it? It's not only unfair, but it's unpredictable. Yet that's the way it is."

Annie blew her nose. Life may be unfair and unpredictable, she thought, but I can still get even though it doesn't bring my dog back. She remembered she once thought her Orphan Annie Code Captain's belt could unlock the secrets of the universe. She was younger then. At least she knew now: Z doesn't equal 1.

The next day at school, Mr. Moore called a special assembly for grades four through twelve. The study hall was so crowded that all the fourth, fifth, and sixth grades had to share desks. This time the twelfth graders sat at the back of the room, and Annie and her friends were scrunched in with the younger kids. Annie turned around to see all the bigger kids behind her. "It's as if we've got leprosy," she said to Margaret, who was sharing a desk with her.

Mr. Moore tapped and tested the microphone. "I've called you here today for a very serious reason. Someone—and we think it's one of you—has been breaking the law."

Immediately, the entire group became alert and attentive.

"With this in mind I want to introduce Mr. Jason Carey, a representative from the FCC—the Federal Communications Commission—who has come all the way from South Bend to speak to you."

Mr. Carey walked confidently to the microphone and with a serious look on his face began to speak.

"The FCC is empowered by the federal government to license and regulate broadcasting stations and to preserve the freedom of these stations to broadcast over their assigned wave lengths. This means that we assign specific frequencies to each radio station, and in turn we make sure that each station can broadcast without illegal interference." He paused and continued in a stern voice. "Someone in this room has been interfering with the rights and freedom of these stations to broadcast."

Margaret nudged Annie with her elbow. Annie stared straight ahead. "That person is subject to a fine and possible imprisonment for breaking the law unless he immediately refrains from his illegal activities."

After they were dismissed, there was much pushing and shoving as students hurried to get a drink of water or talk to a friend before returning to classes. Margaret and Annie were separated in the crowd.

"Annie, Annie, come here, we want to talk to you," called one of the high-school boys whom Annie barely knew.

It was Tom Braden's brother Joe.

She walked over to where he stood with his friends, her insides churning from the words "fine and imprisonment." Surely, no one but Margaret and Bobby knew about the Ford coils, and they wouldn't tell.

"You're the kid who sings outside teachers' windows, aren't you?"

Annie hesitated. "Yes."

"Well, my friends and I have a favor to ask. We want you to sneak into Mr. Wood's chemistry room after school and take a brown bottle off the shelf. It's right inside the door and labeled potassium something or other. I'll draw a map for you and draw a picture of the bottle with the label on it."

Annie was curious and flattered. It wasn't often that a high-school student would be seen talking to a sixth grader.

"What do you want it for?" she asked.

"Well, it's neat stuff. When it's exposed to air, it makes a little explosion. You see, it ties in with some plans we've made."

"But why are you asking me? said Annie.

"'Cause you're a kid. Besides, you're just a girl and no one would suspect you."

Annie thought back to the assembly speaker who said, "he is subject to a fine and possible imprisonment." Then the phrase "Just a girl" echoed in her mind. She looked up and saw Bobby and Margaret watching her anxiously.

"I've got to leave now," she said.

Fortunately, the first bell rang at that moment, signaling time to return to class.

"Remember to keep your mouth shut," hissed Joe as he hurried away.

"What were you doing talking to Joe Braden?" demanded Bobby. "He and his brother are troublemakers."

"We'll be late for class," said Annie, starting to leave.

"Well, I want my Ford coil back today," said Bobby firmly. "I don't want to be fined and go to prison."

When Annie got home for lunch, there was a package and a letter on the dining room table from her cousin John. They were both addressed to her. In his letter John thanked her for the get-well card she had sent him. He wrote that he was feeling much better, and since he hoped to be traveling abroad over the Christmas holidays, he was mailing her gift ahead of time.

"In addition to the enclosed check," he wrote, "I have included a package of crocus bulbs for you to plant on Sandy's grave if you wish. I've had a lot of time to think recently. Please remember when you plant these bulbs that nothing and no one ever really dies—we are just changed. Physically, the remains of Sandy's body will nourish these bulbs which will produce new life in the spring—but more importantly, every time you remember Sandy, he will, in a way, be alive again." Annie thought back to the trip she and her mother had made to the cemetery to decorate her grandparents' grave for Decoration Day. No wonder my cancer skirt upset her, she thought. It reminded her of John's illness. Then, if my cancer skirt can make her sad, I can remember Sandy's life, and remembering can make me happy. But thoughts of Sandy's death, Mr. Sayers, the man from the FCC, and Joe Braden and his strange request pushed and shoved their way into her mind like the students jostling each other on the way out of study hall that morning.

That night the clock in the library downstairs struck ten; all was quiet. This time, along with the tape, Annie put a sealed envelope in her pocket. The neighboring houses weren't quite dark yet when she sneaked out the front door. Both the Karschmans' and Myerses' homes had lights shining from their upstairs windows, but Bobby's room was dark.

She fingered the tape and envelope in her dress pocket and walked down the alley toward the park. When she came to the vacant lot on the west side of the park, she looked around carefully, but she saw no one. Even so, a feeling of dread weighed heavily upon her. Her hands shook as she taped the envelope to the back door of Mr. Sayers's shop.

"That's done," she said to herself. Suddenly a harsh voice immediately behind her said, "Well, Missy, what do you think you're doing?"

Annie sucked in her breath, too startled to scream. Turning around, she found the menacing form of Mr. Sayers looking down at her.

"You. . .you killed my dog, didn't you?" she said.

"Oh, you're the Ziegler kid," replied Mr. Sayers, shining his flashlight in her face.

"You did it, didn't you?"

"Did what?"

"Killed my dog!"

"What?"

"You shot Sandy!"

"What makes you say that?"

"Well, your shop is right here next to the park," said Annie in a shaky voice, "and you hate animals and you were glad Frederick's dog was shot. . . ."

"Little girl, do your parents know where you are? I think I'll just give them a call," said Mr. Sayers, heading for the door of his shop.

"No, wait!" said Annie, trying to keep from crying. "I'm going home, but first I want to know. Are you the one?"

"The one who shot your dog? It's true I don't like animals who run loose, and I was dern glad to see Frederick's dog put away. It had no business running loose to begin with, but I ain't no animal killer. Not that I'm a vegetarian, mind you, but I don't shoot dogs."

"But who did?"

"I don't know for sure, but I ain't the only one who was mad at that critter."

Annie looked up at Mr. Sayers's bearded face and squinty eyes surrounded by wrinkles—all illuminated grotesquely by the flashlight he was holding. She turned as if to go.

"Wait a minute, missy. What about my broken window? You're the one that did it, ain't ya?"

Annie nodded meekly and pointed to the envelope taped on the door.

Mr. Sayers walked over to the door, pulled off the envelope, and tore it open. Inside was a check for five dollars made out to Annie—the Christmas gift from Cousin John. On the opposite side of the check, Annie had written, "Pay to the order of John Sayers" and signed her name.

Mr. Sayers examined the check and its endorsement by the light of his flashlight. Then he read aloud Annie's note: "I still think you killed my dog, but here's the money for your window. 15, 3, 3, 8, 4 (Annie) Ziegler."

When he had finished, Mr. Sayers stroked his beard and looked thoughtful for a long time. Annie stood first on one foot, then the other, waiting to be dismissed.

Finally, Mr. Sayers spoke. "I know I'm a crotchety old man, but you were wrong about me. You cain't always judge a book by its cover, you know." With that, he turned to leave.

"Mr. Sayers," Annie said.

The old man paused.

"I'm sorry."

He nodded and walked away.

Chapter Ten

Sandy's Killer

Saturday was rainy, and Annie moped around the house. Margaret was out of town with her parents, and Bobby was off with his brother. She tried to amuse herself by going through her mother's old magazines and filling out coupons for free samples of Lady Esther Face Powder—five different shades—and Tangee lipstick, which her mother probably wouldn't let her wear because she was "too young."

"Annie, I've got an idea," said her mother, walking into the kitchen where Annie sat at the table cutting out the coupons and addressing envelopes. "Let's go shopping."

Annie looked up with surprise. "OK," she replied, "but what will we buy?"

"For one thing, you need some new shoes."

"What kind of shoes would you like, Annie?" asked her mother when the salesman at Goldberg's approached them.

"Pretty brown ones that fit," replied Annie as the salesman measured her foot.

"Your feet have grown; they're a size larger than these shoes," the salesman said.

After trying on several pairs of shoes, Annie selected a pair quite different from the unworn orthopedic shoes on the floor of her closet. The salesman took the shoes and put them in a box. Then Mrs. Ziegler handed him a five-dollar bill, which he placed in a small cylindrical compartment. After sliding the compartment's door shut, he put the cylinder in a tube. Annie could hear it whooshing all the way across the store's ceiling to the cashier's cage. A few minutes later, it whooshed back with her mother's change.

"Annie, let's walk through the hat department on our way out. Your father and I have decided to go to a medical convention in French Lick over Thanksgiving, and I think I'd like a hat to go with my new brown suit."

Hmmm, Annie thought, that's a change.

Annie saw it first—a brown felt hat with delicate orange and yellow feathers fastened to the band circling the crown of the hat.

"Oh, Mother, get that one. It's beautiful," said Annie.

"Well, it is beautiful, but it's rather showy, I think."

"Try it on," Annie suggested enthusiastically.

Mrs. Ziegler placed the hat on her head carefully.

"Oh, it looks so pretty on," said Annie. "Please buy it."

"Well, it is becoming. I just hope it's not too worldly," said her mother uncertainly, but she handed the hat and three dollars to the hovering saleslady.

"How soon will you wear it?" asked Annie.

"Well, your father offered to stay home a week from tomorrow and answer the phone so that I could go to my church. It's Communion Sunday, and I don't want to miss, so I guess I'll wear it then," she concluded.

Halloween had come and gone. Now it was almost Thanksgiving. Bits of snow stung their faces as Annie and her friends stood outside the GRADE entrance. For once they didn't even avoid the little kids as they all huddled together—hands in pockets—waiting for the morning bell to ring and signal permission to enter the warm building.

"Hey, Annie, come here," called Joe Braden as he invited her into the warm vestibule at the HIGH entrance—

a small space available only to the students big enough and tough enough to fight for it.

Annie was cold, and to the astonishment of her friends and the envy of her acquaintances, she accepted Joe's offer. The crowd of big kids surrounding the HIGH entrance made way for Joe as he led Annie in the warm entryway. Once there, he ordered everyone else out. Then he reached into his pocket and pulled out two pieces of paper.

"Here's the map showing the location of the bottles in the chemistry room. Now all you've got to do. . . ."

Annie interrupted with the speech she had been planning to give for the past week. "I may be just a girl to you, but I've outgrown that kid stuff!"

Joe's eyes opened wide and his face grew red. "If I had my brother's rifle, you wouldn't be talking about kid stuff," he snarled.

"Your brother's rifle?" Suddenly, Annie became very still and white. "Your brother, Tom, killed my dog, didn't he?"

"Why don't you ask him?" stammered Joe, realizing he had said too much.

"I will," said Annie as she turned and left.

"But Annie," said Bobby that day at recess, "Tom Braden is big and mean."

"I know," replied Annie looking from Bobby to Margaret as the three crowded together in a corner of the building not exposed to the cold November wind.

"Are you sure he killed Sandy?" asked Margaret, her teeth chattering from the cold.

"Yes, I'm sure," replied Annie. "When I asked Mr. Sayers if he knew who killed my dog, he said he wasn't the only one with a reason. This morning I remembered that Sandy brought a dead rabbit home with one of Tom's traps still attached to it."

"Nobody else 'round here is mean enough to trap rabbits," said Bobby.

"Or poor enough," added Margaret.

"And when Joe let it slip that his brother had a rifle, I just knew it was Tom," said Annie. "Plus the funny way Joe acted when I accused his brother."

"OK," said Bobby with a sigh. "Right after school, I'll get the rifle shell and meet you two in front of the Bradens' house."

The wind was banging the gate to the unpainted fence that enclosed the Bradens' small yard when the three friends met that afternoon. Determined, Annie led the way up to the front door, which was also in need of paint. Since there was no doorbell, she took off her mitten and rapped on the door with her clenched fist.

The door opened and Mrs. Braden stood in front of them wearing a faded housedress, a baby clutched in her left arm.

"Yes?" she asked expectantly.

Annie noticed her face was wrinkled and tired. "I'm Annie Ziegler and these are my friends, Bobby and Margaret." Annie's voice trembled. She cleared her throat. "We'd like to talk to Tom."

"Come in," said Mrs. Braden quietly, leading the way into the dark living room, which was furnished with only a shabby couch and two straight-backed chairs.

"Tom," she called into a back room.

Annie hardly recognized Tom Braden when the teenager came in the room. His scowl was gone, and in its place was a worried look.

Remaining in the room, Mrs. Braden shifted the baby to her other arm and waited.

Annie reached into the pocket of her coat and pulled

out the rifle shell. "Is this yours?" she asked, holding it up for Tom to see.

Tom looked uneasy and glanced at his mother. "It might be," he said. Taking a step forward, he took a closer look.

Annie looked at Bobby and Margaret for support. "Did you kill my dog?" she asked in a low firm voice.

Tom looked at his mother. Then he blurted out, "I didn't mean to kill it. I just meant to wound it or scare it off. It was taking my rabbits. . .and we needed them."

"Oh, Tom," his mother said.

"But Ma, we did," said Tom desperately.

"I know," said his mother, "but killing a little girl's dog. . . ."

Tom looked at Annie. "I'm sorry, honest I am."

Annie felt defeated. Somehow she had thought that knowing Sandy's killer would help, but it didn't. Her dog was still dead. She turned and stumbled towards the door. Margaret and Bobby followed, saying a hurried good-bye to Mrs. Braden on their way out.

That night at dinner Annie told her parents about the visit to the Bradens' house and about her earlier conversation with Mr. Sayers, skipping over the parts about the notes and broken window.

She ended her story by recounting in detail her conversation with Tom Braden and his apology. "But that doesn't bring my dog back," she concluded bitterly.

"No, it doesn't," her father said. "But you did enjoy Sandy when he was alive, didn't you?"

"Yes," Annie replied, thinking of Cousin John's letter.

"Do you think Tom was really sorry?" Annie asked after a pause.

"I think he was," answered Mrs. Ziegler. "We often do things we're sorry about afterward."

"Knowing the Bradens, Tom won't be using that rifle for a long time—if ever," said Dr. Ziegler. "Annie," he continued, "You were brave to go to Tom's house and speak to him. I know some adults who wouldn't have had the courage to do that."

Annie looked at her father gratefully. "I hadn't thought of that," she said.

There was a long silence. Finally Mrs. Ziegler said quietly, "I know how disappointed you are. I want to tell you both about my own disappointment. It happened on Communion Sunday. The bishop was at church that day." She paused, then sighed and continued. "And he wouldn't let me take communion."

"Why not?" asked Annie, bewildered.

"Because of my hat."

"The new one with the pretty orange and yellow feathers?"

"Yes. He said it was too worldly and that I was disobeying a rule of the church by wearing it. I hadn't the courage to tell you before."

"What a dumb rule," Annie said without thinking.

Her mother looked at her sharply. "Well, it is a rule, and if I'm going to be a member of that church, I have to follow it." Then she sighed again. "But I don't see how wearing it can be so wrong."

On the Wednesday before Thanksgiving, grades one through six presented a Thanksgiving pageant for the older students. All the junior high and senior high students gathered in the study hall and faced a stage decorated with shocks of corn and a backdrop upon which the art students had painted a Pilgrim hut. In the middle of the stage were three long sticks placed together teepee fashion. From the center of the sticks was suspended a black cauldron on a chain. Underneath the cauldron a red cellophane "fire" burned, powered by hidden flashlights. Mrs. Diller, who had generously forgiven Annie, and Mrs. Wingrab were backstage shushing everyone and making last-minute adjustments on Pilgrims' collars and Indians' feathers.

Annie, Bobby, and Margaret were all cast as Pilgrims. At first, Bobby wanted to be the turkey, then an Indian, but finally Mrs. Wingrab talked him into taking the role of Governor Bradford. He wore a black crepe-paper suit, white stockings, a black cardboard hat, and gold cardboard shoe buckles.

The elementary choir—grades one through four—began the program with "Over the river and through the woods to Grandfather's house we go. . . ." Next the fifth and sixth graders took over.

Margaret, wearing a long black dress with a white collar and a white cap, came out on the stage and began reading.

"On a bright November day in 1621 Governor William Bradford proclaimed a three-day festival to commemorate that fall's bountiful harvest," she began in a clear voice.

At the mention of Governor Bradford, Bobby made his entrance on stage. He held a big sheet of paper rolled into a scroll, from which he pretended to read.

Margaret continued. "Joining the celebration that year was Chief Massasoit and his tribe who, temporarily at peace with the white man, brought with them wild turkeys as part of their contribution to the feast."

At this point Dan Ramshaw entered, covered with greasepaint and wearing a magnificent Indian headdress used by the basketball team's mascot whenever the Wakarusa Indians had a game. With him was little Monty Riesenberger, dressed as a turkey, his feathers made out of colored construction paper and stapled onto a cardboard tail.

The audience laughed when they saw Monty. Backstage, Annie, watching through a hole in the scenery, saw that even Mr. Warman smiled along with them.

"Beset with disease and disaster," Margaret read on, "our Pilgrim fathers and mothers managed to overcome these unpredictable events and, because of their tenacity, courage, and perseverance, faced the unknown future bravely while helping found our country."

From her position at the peephole, Annie heard someone next to her muttering. It was Arnie Peterson, one of the few black students at school. "They weren't my fathers and mothers," he said.

Annie whispered to him, "It's our turn to go on stage."

Annie and two other Pilgrims grouped themselves on one side of the stage, while Arnie and three additional Indians arranged themselves on the other for the climax of the pageant.

Chief Massasoit stepped forward, shaking his head slightly to show off his splendid headdress. "Why, O great one," he said, addressing Governor Bradford, "have you come to these lands?"

"To seek freedom," replied the governor. For once, Bobby was being very serious.

"Freedom. What is that?" asked the chief.

"Freedom is many things to many people," replied the governor. "But for us it is the opportunity to worship God as we please without fear of punishment or restraint."

"Ah," replied the chief. "We Indians were free to worship the Great Spirit as we saw fit long before the white man arrived."

"Let us join hands then," said the governor, "to show that we respect one another's beliefs and to show that this nation has always cherished freedom."

While Mrs. Diller played "We gather together to ask the Lord's blessing," the remaining fifth and sixth graders, dressed as Pilgrims or Indians, marched on stage hand in hand. Then everyone, including the turkey, sang "America, the Beautiful."

When it was all over, Mr. Moore stood up and thanked them, asking Mrs. Diller, Mrs. Wingrab, and Margaret to take a bow. All the junior high and senior high students applauded as the Pilgrims and Indians shook hands and marched off the stage.

When Annie came home from school that day, both of her parents were packed and ready to leave for the medical convention in French Lick.

Nora was busy unpacking her suitcase, for she was going to stay with Annie while her parents were gone. She'd be there for Thanksgiving. Annie didn't mind a bit that her parents would be gone. She liked being with Nora.

"Did you buy the ham?" Annie asked her mother.

"Yes, and Nora has baked you an angel food cake with caramel icing just as you asked."

"Oh, boy, a Thanksgiving dinner without chicken or turkey!" said Annie. "What a treat!"

Dr. Ziegler turned to kiss his daughter good-bye.

"Wait, a minute. I want to get something," said Mrs. Ziegler, hurrying back to their bedroom. When she came out, she had on the brown hat with the yellow and orange feathers.

"Some rules are dumb," she said to Annie as she kissed her.

After her parents left, Annie took an oblong object wrapped in damp newspaper plus the bag of crocus bulbs from John and went to the woodshed, where she found a trowel. Then she knelt down in front of the small mound of dirt in her father's garden. Sandy's grave. Carefully she dug four holes, each three or four inches deep. In each hole she arranged three crocus bulbs in the shape of a triangle. Then she covered the holes with dirt. When she had finished, she smoothed the dirt over the top of the mound and unwrapped the package. Inside the damp paper was a rose—"The last rose of summer," Nora had called it when she had given it to Annie earlier. Somehow, in its protected spot behind the chicken coop on Nora's farm, the lovely pink rose had escaped the frost. Now, on the day before Thanksgiving, it was blooming. Annie gently placed it on Sandy's grave as John's words came to her mind—"Every time you remember Sandy, he will, in a way, be alive again." Then she stood up and went into the house.

Suddenly, she realized that since the time of Sandy's death, she had been imprisoned in a dark and painful tunnel, more scary than the one at Bobby's Halloween party, and one from which she had tried to escape by getting even with Mr. Sayers and getting in trouble at school. But recently she had begun to emerge. She was now free. There would be other tunnels in life to go through, yet somehow she knew that she'd get through them. She hadn't unlocked the secrets of the universe, but she had discovered that Z is not always equal to 1.

That night she dreamed of a meadow filled with wildflowers and animals romping freely. In the distance, she thought she saw the graceful brown horse and Sandy.

Chapter Eleven

Thanksgiving Day

On Thanksgiving Day Annie woke to the delicious smell of ham cooking. Looking out the window, she saw there had been a hard frost. The grass, covered with millions of ice crystals, sparkled in the sunlight.

Just for the fun of it, she made her bed and brushed her hair. After dressing, she went downstairs and found Nora at the kitchen table drinking coffee.

"I heard you get up, Annie, so I heated your Ovaltine," she said, pouring it into a coffee mug like hers.

They sat quietly sipping their hot drinks. Then Nora got up to clear the table.

"I'll do the dishes," said Annie.

"Thanks," Nora said. "That way I can get your father's paperwork done sooner."

As Nora went out the back door to Dr. Ziegler's office, Annie heard someone on the front porch. She looked through the window at the top of the door. It was Bobby. She opened the door, and there he stood with a puppy in his arms.

"Look, Annie, my brother and I got it last night. We're going to build a pen for it, and when it gets bigger, my dad will put up a fence."

Annie opened her mouth, but no words came out.

Bobby didn't seem to notice. "I've got a collar and a new leash. Let's take it for a walk."

Annie ran to get her jacket. When she returned, Bobby

put the pup down and together they watched it waddle down the front steps.

She smiled. So cute. Almost as cute as a bug's ear.

She looked at Bobby. Somehow he appeared different—taller and slimmer.

"You're the first person I've told," she said, "but from now on I want to be called Ann."

"OK, Ann," he said, and his blue eyes twinkled like the shimmering grass at their feet.

Acknowledgments

I am very grateful to Mark, Scott, and Cindy Shoemaker for their technical, artistic, and proof-reading contributions. My gratitude extends to Carol Elrod, who encouraged me and introduced me to Hawthorne Publishing and to Art and Nancy Baxter of Hawthorne Publishing, without whose help this book would not have been possible.

Finally, I want to acknowledge the many people in Wakarusa who were kind to children and taught us the real value of community. Indeed, it does take a village to raise a child.